Groundwood Books is grateful for the opportunity to share stories and make books on the Traditional Territory of many Nations, including the Anishinabeg, the Wendat and the Haudenosaunee. It is also the Treaty Lands of the Mississaugas of the Credit. In partnership with Indigenous writers, illustrators, editors and translators, we commit to publishing stories that reflect the experiences of Indigenous Peoples. For more about our work and values, visit us at groundwoodbooks.com.

ONE MORE MOUNTAIN

ONE MORE MOUNTAIN

DEBORAH ELLIS

Groundwood Books
House of Anansi Press
Toronto / Berkeley

Published in 2022 by Groundwood Books / House of Anansi Press
groundwoodbooks.com

We gratefully acknowledge for their financial support of our publishing program the Canada Council for the Arts, the Ontario Arts Council and the Government of Canada.

 Canada Council
for the Arts
Conseil des Arts
du Canada

 ONTARIO ARTS COUNCIL
CONSEIL DES ARTS DE L'ONTARIO
an Ontario government agency
un organisme du gouvernement de l'Ontario

With the participation of the Government of Canada
Avec la participation du gouvernement du Canada | **Canadä**

Library and Archives Canada Cataloguing in Publication
Title: One more mountain / Deborah Ellis.
Names: Ellis, Deborah, author.
Series: Ellis, Deborah, Breadwinner series.
Description: Series statement: Breadwinner series.
Identifiers: Canadiana (print) 20220132461 | Canadiana (ebook) 2022013247X | ISBN 9781773068855 (hardcover) | ISBN 9781773068862 (EPUB)
Classification: LCC PS8559.L5494 O54 2022 | DDC jC813/.54—dc23

Jacket illustration by Aurélia Fronty
Design by Michael Solomon
Printed and bound in Canada

Groundwood Books is a Global Certified Accessible™ (GCA by Benetech) publisher. An ebook version of this book that meets stringent accessibility standards is available to students and readers with print disabilities.

Groundwood Books is committed to protecting our natural environment. This book is made of material from well-managed FSC®-certified forests, recycled materials and other controlled sources.

 MIX
Paper from
responsible sources
FSC® C103567

To those who keep climbing,
long past when they should have to.

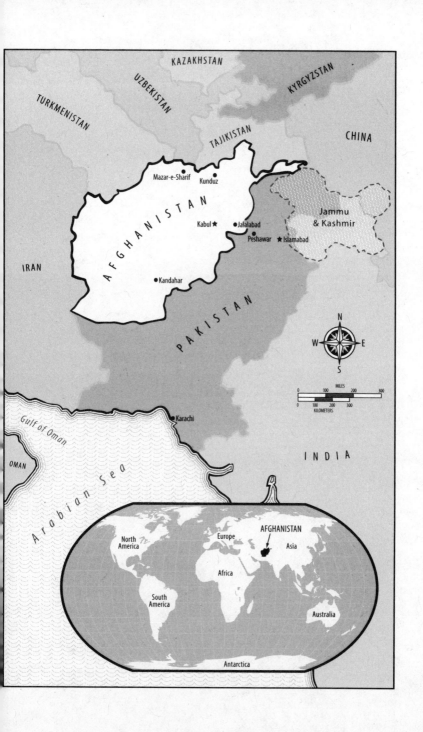

1

"No one can help me," Damsa said. "You can't help me."

She teetered at the very edge of the roof of the ruined building.

"I really can." The policewoman stood on the roof behind her. She took a step toward the girl.

"It's no good," Damsa said. A shuffle of her feet sent stones tumbling down three stories to the broken concrete chunks below. "My father wants to kill me."

"Yes, I imagine he does." The policewoman took two more steps forward. "There are men who want to kill me, too."

She held out her hand toward Damsa, and actually smiled.

"But they'll have to find us, first."

2

Damsa peered through the screen covering her eyes. She had never worn a burqa before, but the officer had taken two out of the police car, pulled one over her own head and insisted Damsa wear the other one.

"It will be safer for both of us."

It was also safer for them to abandon the police car in the weeds by the ruined house where Damsa had almost jumped off the roof.

"The Taliban are hunting down women in uniform," the police officer told her.

They walked for three hours, ducking and hiding each time a pickup truck full of Taliban soldiers drove along the highway.

Now, finally, they had arrived.

"We're here."

High gray walls framed a large, bright pink gate decorated with painted flowers in orange, blue and yellow.

Damsa read the name on the gate.

Green Valley.

The policewoman pressed the buzzer and then flipped back her burqa so that the eyes on the other side of the small opening could see her face. Damsa heard a bolt slide back. The door in the gate was swung open by a girl Damsa's age.

"Shauzia!" A boy around eleven let go of the big suitcase that he'd been pulling toward a car in the courtyard. He ran to the policewoman and gave her a giant hug.

"I thought you wouldn't get here on time," he said.

"Do you really think I'd let you go to the other side of the world without a proper goodbye from me?" Shauzia asked. "Rafi, I should arrest you for even thinking that."

Rafi laughed.

"Maryam's giving Mama a hard time," he said.

"Another day at the office, then." Shauzia hugged Rafi close again. Then he ran off across the yard.

"Mama! Shauzia's here!"

"I'm glad you made it," said the girl who had let them in the gate.

"Not half as glad as I am," said the officer. "This is Damsa."

"Hello, Damsa," the girl said. "I'm Larmina. I'll get you something to eat."

She left them in the yard.

Officer Shauzia led Damsa to a bench in the yard under a tree.

"You can take off the burqa," she said.

Damsa was relieved to sit. She'd been on the run for days, with no food and very little water. She'd been too afraid to sleep much.

Now that she was seated, she was too tired to even lift the burqa from her face. The policewoman did it for her.

Larmina brought a tray with water, dates and walnuts and left it on a little table beside the bench. Shauzia poured Damsa a drink and handed her the glass, then poured herself some water and sat down beside her.

"Welcome to Green Valley," Officer Shauzia said, and drained her glass.

Damsa tried to raise her glass to her lips but her hand was shaking. She used both hands and took a long drink.

She looked around at where she was.

There was color everywhere. So much color that the rest of the world Damsa had known seemed dull and dusty by comparison. The bright whitewashed walls around the compound were covered in designs and murals. Carpets and quilts aired in the sunshine.

Even the bench she was sitting on was painted light blue with purple irises.

Many gardens bloomed. Tidy pathways wove between the gardens, leading to a one-story main house and several smaller outbuildings toward the back. The main house had a large awning for protection from the sun and the rain.

The whole place was neat and yet a bit messy and full of life.

The courtyard at Damsa's father's house had been all gray stone, meticulously swept by servants who scurried away like frightened mice whenever a member of the household or a guest appeared. Her father liked the help to stay out of the way.

A woman with a straight back and a determined jaw came out of the main building, took two steps toward Shauzia, then turned back and called through the open door.

"Maryam, if you are not out here in five minutes, they are leaving without you!"

"I don't know why you shout at her, Parvana," said Shauzia, leaving the bench and crossing the yard to her. "You know it does no good."

"They have to be at the safe house before dark," Parvana said. She and Shauzia loaded the big suitcase the boy had been pulling into the open trunk of the car. "I won't have them on the road after dark."

"I'm sure Asif knows that," said Shauzia.

"You're sure I know what?"

A man on crutches, an empty trouser leg neatly pinned up, came into the yard with two backpacks over his shoulders.

"I'm sure you know not to cause your wife extra worry."

"That I do know," he said, tossing the two packs into the car's back seat. "How bad is it out there?"

"There are Taliban on the highway," said Officer Shauzia, "but if you stick to the back roads, you should make it to Kabul without a problem."

"Inshallah," he said. "Princess Maryam is on her way out."

"Soon she'll be Nooria's problem," said Parvana. She put her arms around Rafi. Asif joined them in the embrace.

A voice called from the house.

"I am here. I am ready. I couldn't find my gold. I turned all my music earnings into gold chains to take with me, but I couldn't find them. Then I remembered they are already around my neck."

A woman, younger than Parvana and Shauzia, and much more beautifully dressed in an elaborately embroidered tunic, came into the yard pulling a small suitcase.

"I don't know why we have to leave so early," the woman said. "Our flight doesn't leave until midday tomorrow."

Damsa nearly dropped her glass of water. She couldn't believe what she was seeing! All exhaustion fell away as she got to her feet and practically flew across the yard.

"You're Maryam Gulalai," she said. "You're Maryam Gulalai! I know all your songs!"

Maryam's face went from annoyed and flustered to smiling and gracious.

"Aren't you kind?" she said, adjusting her chador so that it draped more elegantly. "What is your name?"

"Damsa. I...I did a YouTube video of me singing one of your songs, 'Almond Trees in Bloom.' Did you see it?"

"I'll look it up when I'm in the airport," Maryam said. "Goodness knows I'll have lots of time." She glared at Parvana.

"Get in the car, Maryam," said Parvana, but when Maryam started to do that, Parvana grabbed her and hugged her. "I love you and I am so proud of you," Damsa heard her say.

Damsa felt herself shoved out of the way as other girls rushed out of the house and into the yard, all saying goodbye and crying. She went back to her bench. Shauzia got the girls through their farewells and back inside the house.

Then it was just Parvana, Rafi, Asif and Maryam left by the car.

Rafi started to cry.

"Mama! Don't make me go! I don't want to go!"

Parvana knelt down so she could look him in the eye. "Yes, you do. You want to go and become a famous Afghan ballet dancer. You will show all those students at that school what it means to work hard and dream big. You will create dances of such beauty that people will look at them and say, 'That is Afghanistan!' And if you decide that dancing is not for you, that is fine with me because whatever you do, you will be a good, kind man. And your father and I will get our visas and will be visiting you in New York before you know it."

Shauzia came back outside carrying a battered shoulder bag, which she handed to Parvana. Parvana held it up to Rafi.

"You know what this is," she said to him. "It belonged to my father, your grandfather. I carried it when I went with him to the market to read letters for people who couldn't read for themselves. Then, after he died, I had it with me when I met your father in a cave, back when we were children not much older than you." She put it over his shoulder "We will always be with you," she said.

She stood up, nodded at Shauzia, and Shauzia got the boy into the front seat of the car.

"You get them safely through the airport and then you drive right back here. You hear me, Asif?"

"Parvana, the general," he joked. "Always giving orders." He got in the car and closed the door. "I won't let anything bad happen to our son."

"What about to me?" Damsa heard Maryam ask from the back seat.

"You, I'm feeding to the wild dogs, first chance I get. And put that burqa on. Your fans might want to see your face but the Taliban certainly does not."

The car started up. Shauzia opened the gate. And then they were gone.

Officer Shauzia closed the gate and stood beside Parvana. Damsa watched them cry.

Damsa's eyes got heavier and heavier, and then they just closed.

3

"You should give the tickets to me."

Maryam stuck her hand between the front seats and waggled her fingers.

"Mama said no."

"And I say yes. I'm the adult here. You're a child. It's humiliating to have my passport carried by an eight-year-old."

Rafi looked at his father who was driving the car. Asif looked back at him with a quick smile.

"I'm eleven," said Rafi.

"Give them to me and I'll buy a motorcycle when we get to New York and give you a ride on it every day."

"Mama said I was to keep all the documents," said Rafi. "She also said I can't ride on a motorcycle until I'm fifty."

"Well, Parvana might be the boss of you but she is not the boss of me," said Maryam.

"Parvana is, was and forever shall be the boss of all of us," said Asif.

"Ridiculous." Maryam bumped back in her seat with frustration. "I'm a music superstar and my older sister still thinks she can run my life. Well, she won't be able to do that when I'm in New York."

"No," said Rafi's father. "Nooria will."

Rafi burst out laughing. He'd never met his Aunt Nooria, but he'd heard the stories. He came from a family of bossy women.

The drive to Kabul usually took three hours. They'd been driving for four already and they still had a long way to go. It was stop, then start, then stop again.

Rafi stuck his legs out in front of him, stretching his muscles.

"We'll stop soon to take a break," his father said.

Not long after that, they drove up to a gas station. As the attendant filled the tank and checked the oil, Rafi helped his father to the restroom. Asif could usually manage fine on his crutches, but his muscles were stiff and sore from the drive.

Maryam complained about the dirtiness of the place.

"You can sit here and continue to complain or you can use the facilities, but not both," Asif said. "Because we're driving away in five minutes, whether or not you are back in the car."

Rafi started to stretch and bend. He held the side of the car as if it was a ballet barre, but his father stopped him.

"Do nothing to draw attention," Asif said, and Rafi knew his father was right. He jogged in place instead.

When Aunt Maryam reappeared, he helped her get back in the car. She was not used to the burqa. Rafi's mother had tried to get her to wear it around the compound to get used to it, but Maryam had only done that once, and just for a moment.

"I can't see, I can't breathe, and no one can see my face," Maryam had whined. "This is 2021, Parvana. You think we're still living in the dark ages."

Parvana had not replied to that. And now Maryam was not used to the burqa that covered her entire body like a tent. She was uncomfortable, she was unhappy, and she made sure everyone knew it.

Finally, Asif told her, "You leave it on or I'm taking you home and giving your visa and ticket to Parvana."

Maryam's complaints weren't quite so loud after that.

"What if she won't do what she needs to do at the airport?" Rafi asked his father quietly, hoping his voice would be blocked by his aunt's burqa and the sound of the car going over the rough road.

"Do your best to get her though the security check and to the waiting area for your flight," his father said. "Ask an airport worker for help if you need it. If she continues to be impossible, let her have her ticket and her papers and let her manage herself. Your job is to get yourself on the plane. Your aunt is a grown-up. At some point, she has to be responsible for herself."

It was an old argument between his parents—Parvana insisting that Maryam needed her help, always had and always would, and Asif saying Parvana needed to help Maryam more than Maryam needed help from Parvana. And that as soon as Parvana realized that, Maryam would start to stand on her own two feet.

Rafi thought they were both right. Maryam *could* look after herself, but he doubted that she ever would.

It wasn't just that Maryam was selfish. It was that she truly believed that what *she* wanted to do at any particular moment was more important than what anyone else wanted her to do.

"Other people will eat away your life," she had told Rafi on more than one occasion. "I want to sing, so that has to be first. If I paid attention to your mother, she'd have me sweeping floors and bathing rescued babies all day. Claim your time! Your art is important!"

Yes, his art — his dancing — was important, Rafi believed. It was also important that he learn from his father how to fix a car so he could get it going again if it broke down on the way to a performance, and to know how to cook for himself and grow food and chop wood and keep his clothes clean. He told Maryam that once.

"No, no, no. You've got it all wrong," she said. "If you do those things one time, they'll make you do them all the time. Better to plead incompetence and make other people do things for you. Then you can concentrate on your art."

Parvana never let Maryam get away with that kind of behavior, but it was always a struggle.

Exasperating as she was, Rafi could never be completely fed up with his Aunt Maryam. After all, she was the reason he was dancing, and she was the reason he was going to New York.

Years ago, when Rafi was little, he was sitting with Maryam as she searched the internet for dance moves she could do while she sang. She passed right by the video of the boy spinning and leaping across a stage.

"Go back! Go back!" Rafi had ordered. He watched, jaw open, as a boy just a little bit bigger than him used movement alone to become a bird, then a lion, then something else altogether, twisting and flying, not bound by gravity.

He watched the video ten times, and then another ten, and at least ten times a day after that, day after day after day.

It was Aunt Maryam who found ballet lessons online and taught him the five positions. It was Aunt Maryam who got his father to build him a ballet barre, and Aunt Maryam who, after years of him learning and practicing, sent a video of him dancing to Aunt Nooria in New York. Aunt Nooria used that video to get him a scholarship to a ballet school in New York City.

For one year, he would be a provisional student under their International Opportunities program.

He would live with Nooria and spend his days at the school getting proper dance training as well as regular school lessons. If they liked him, they would let him stay.

Rafi watched Afghanistan move past the car window.

In his head, he was dancing.

He danced on the flat rooftops of buildings being constructed and buildings that had been bombed. He leapt from rooftop to rooftop, from mansions to mud-brick huts, from walnut trees to billboards advertising everything from cell phones to biscuits.

He'd heard that in New York City, a person could travel whole city blocks by jumping from one roof to another.

He would do that when he got there. He would definitely do that.

In his mind, Rafi danced in the swirling red dust and up and down the rocky hills. He danced on the wrecks of cars and the skeletons of abandoned military tanks, and he danced with a balloon seller who always seemed to show up just when someone needed to smile.

He would miss his parents like fire, but he would not let that stop him from squeezing every drop of opportunity out of this experience.

In Afghanistan, many boys his age worked all day, crushing rocks or hauling water up hills or selling things in the street or begging. He had met these boys when he went out with his mother as they took food around to homes that had none.

Those boys were just like him, except that they knew hunger better than they knew how to read.

Maryam might think she was special.

Rafi knew that he was not special.

Just lucky.

All three of them let out big sighs of relief when they pulled up in front of the gate of the safe house, a place that took in people who were working for justice and kept them hidden from the authorities.

It was a two-story gray concrete building in a neighborhood full of gray concrete buildings. Rafi had been there just once before, when his parents brought him to Kabul to see the city a few years ago. He remembered how enormous and full of wonders Kabul had been—museums and cafés, massive parks, so many shops, and even an amusement park!

One day, he would come back and see it all again.

Rafi got out of the car and pressed the buzzer. He spoke to a man on the other side of the gate.

"We are friends of Mrs. Weera," Rafi said.

The gate swung open and Asif drove the car into a small cement yard.

As soon as the gate was bolted shut, a swarm of people surrounded them, welcoming them and embracing them. Maryam flung back her burqa, happily signed autographs and promised to sing after supper.

Rafi spent the evening eating traditional Kabuli rice and ashak dumplings. He knew it was the last Afghan meal he would have in his home country for a long, long time. He would not be back until he was a man, a professional dancer, ready to set up his Afghan School of Ballet, the biggest of his big dreams.

The people in the safe house had worked with Parvana and Shauzia for a long time. They told stories of Rafi's mother rescuing girls from forced marriages and women from abusive ones, of getting food to families and getting families to doctors, of standing up to corrupt officials and making daring escapes in the night. Mrs. Weera had been a Member of Parliament. His mother and father and Shauzia had lived with her when they were younger, studying as much as they could in between getting other people to safety.

His aunt began to sing—her own hits first, then folk songs. Someone brought out tabla drums and someone else played a rubab lute. Rafi clapped and sang with the others.

When Aunt Maryam started to sing lullabies, he dropped off to sleep.

4

Damsa opened her eyes and saw feet.

Six little feet, not very far from her face.

She closed her eyes again.

She had a vague memory of being led indoors and a vague memory of lowering herself to a toshak.

After that, she remembered nothing.

She heard a giggle.

"You're drooling," piped a young voice.

Damsa was awake now. She fully opened her eyes and stared back at the three little girls. They all had rosy cheeks and laughing eyes. They were sitting right next to her and grinning.

She pushed herself into a sitting position and wiped her mouth. She *had* been drooling.

"What are you staring at?"

"You," said a child, and they all giggled again.

"It's rude to stare," Damsa said.

She couldn't think of anything else to say. She felt that she had been deeply asleep for a long time but had no idea how long or even exactly where she was.

"You're awake."

Larmina stood in the doorway.

"For goodness' sake, girls," she said, "give her some room. You look like a pack of wolves."

The little girls howled and backed away, a little.

"I'm Larmina," she said to Damsa. "We met earlier, but maybe you forgot. This is Damsa, everyone. No, don't tell her your names right now. She won't remember and there is chopping to be done in the kitchen if any of you want to eat tonight. Shoo!"

The little girls shooed, howling and laughing.

"I'm fifteen," said Larmina. "Are you fifteen, too?"

Damsa nodded. Larmina plopped down on the toshak next to her and kept on talking.

"Finally, a girl my own age! I'm sure you're quite beautiful under all that grime. I look okay, but I have these scars on my neck, see?" Larmina moved her scarf to reveal old burn scars, the skin wrinkled and discolored. "My older brother threw hot oil on me when I refused to marry the man my father picked out for me. He tried to get my face but I turned away in time. Parvana says my scar is my badge of honor and I should wear it proudly. Sometimes I can do that. More than I used to, anyway."

Larmina flipped the scarf back around her neck and continued talking.

"I share a room with Hadiah. She's eleven, she thinks. The next oldest to me is Zahra. She's thirteen, but she's got her baby, and she likes to spend time with the three sisters—the wolf pack who was just here—more than with me. They're a lot younger than her but she wants to feel young, I guess, well, who can blame her? Plus, they all want me to act the part of stern older sister so they can be the carefree younger sisters and avoid responsibility. Have you ever studied psychology? Parvana found me some textbooks. It's very interesting, why people do what they do."

"Baby?" asked Damsa. She was struggling to keep up.

"Zahra's the only one of us with a baby," Larmina said. "She was pregnant when she got here, poor thing. Shauzia delivered the baby! I didn't know police officers could do that."

Larmina stood up and offered Damsa her hand.

"Let's get you cleaned up."

There were three stalls in the shower room. An undersea mural was painted on one wall—fish and seaweed and seahorses. There were mirrors over each of the three sinks.

"I'll fetch you some clean clothes and put them on this bench. You can wear some of mine until we get some made for you. The water never gets very hot, but the soap is nice. We make our own. The shampoo, too."

Larmina left her alone.

Damsa looked at her face in the mirror.

It was not a face she knew.

The face she knew was pampered and lotioned, dusted with makeup and glowing with confidence.

The face that stared back at her now was filthy and tired. The heavy makeup her stepmother had plastered on her was smeared with tears and sweat.

It was a face to be shunned, not one to sing on YouTube.

With trembling hands, Damsa undid the buttons on her ruffled white dress.

Her fancy, borrowed engagement dress.

She had been imprisoned inside it for days.

Damsa hated the dress and all it stood for. She ripped herself out of it, tossed it to the floor and got into the shower.

The soap smelled like flowers. The shampoo was smooth. She soaped and rinsed, soaped and rinsed.

She stepped out of the shower stall to clean towels and a faded but pretty yellow and blue shalwar kameez.

She had just finished dressing when Larmina came in.

"I don't want that anymore," Damsa said, pointing to the dress. "Will one of the servants pick it up or do I take it to them?"

"No servants here," said Larmina. "Only queens. And I have a better idea."

She left but came right back, carrying a pair of scissors.

"Cut it up," she said, handing the scissors to Damsa. "We can use the cloth for other things. Cut it up, we'll wash it, and give it a new and happier life."

Damsa took hold of the scissors. She picked up the engagement dress and sat down on the bench.

She thought about how stunned she had been when her stepmother had brought the dress to her in her bedroom.

"You're going to be married," her stepmother said. "Isn't this a pretty dress? You wouldn't know it was used before. I sewed on these ruffles myself."

"Go away," Damsa had said, scrolling through her phone. "I'm busy."

In a split second, her stepmother jerked away the phone and plopped the dress in Damsa's lap.

"You don't speak to me like that, not ever again," her stepmother said. "The day after tomorrow, you will get engaged. Two weeks after that, you will be married. Your father will clear his debt with this marriage, and I will get you out of this house."

Damsa threw the dress to the floor. Her stepmother picked it up and pressed it into Damsa.

"I took trouble to make this look pretty for you," she said. "Is it too much to expect a thank-you? And what other future did you have planned? Did you really think he would keep paying for you forever?"

"Give me my phone back."

"My phone now," her stepmother had said before leaving the room and locking the door.

Oh, how Damsa had pounded! Hours and hours of pounding and kicking and screaming.

When her father finally opened her door, he hit her across the head so hard she fell back onto the expensive carpet. He stood over her, hands on his hips, and she finally saw what others saw.

This was a man who got his way.

Damsa went quiet after that, too shocked and heartbroken for any more fight. She silently watched him strip her room of all the jewelry, fine clothes and the collection of delicate blue glass vases he'd bought for her over the years. He did not say one more word to her as he left the room and locked the door behind him.

For two days she stayed in her room, refusing to eat the food that was brought to her.

The day of the engagement party, her stepmother came into her room.

"It will be fine," her stepmother said, as she pushed Damsa's arms into the sleeves of the dress and smeared makeup on her face. "All the things your father's done for you. You should be happy to do this little thing for him."

Damsa was dressed, painted and perfumed, then left alone while her stepmother went out to greet the guests.

That's when Damsa got over her shock.

And got mad.

She pried open the window lock. She took a long jump into a scratchy shrub. Then she ran away with no money, no papers, no food and no water. Nothing but this fussy, horrible, stifling dress.

Now, as Larmina watched, she cut off a sleeve. Her next cut took off the collar. Then another sleeve.

Then she started to cry.

"I thought my father loved me," she sobbed.

He had been happy to buy her the nice things she wanted. He'd been proud of her good grades in school and her hopes to work in a laboratory one day. She had even shown him the picture she'd drawn of herself in a white lab coat, her hair arranged in a side pony-tail, neat and professional and stylish.

"I'll be a famous scientist during the day and a famous singer at night," she told him.

He had smiled and nodded.

Had he been arranging her marriage even then?

"Just because someone loves us, doesn't mean we have to do everything they want us to do," said Larmina. She took the scissors and the remains of the dress. With quick cuts, she turned it into big pieces and useable scraps. "We'll turn this into dolls, clothes for the baby, bookmarks to sell, many things. Out of something bad, we will make something good."

Out of something bad, something good.

Maybe that can work for me, too, Damsa thought.

5

"Come on. I'll give you the tour."

Larmina took Damsa into the sewing room first. It held pedal sewing machines, two cutting tables and see-through plastic containers filled with fabric and supplies. Larmina left the scissors on one of the tables.

In the laundry porch, they dropped the fabric pieces in a bin with other things that needed washing. Clean clothes hung there from lines stretched post to post. Scrubbing boards leaned against the wall, ready for use.

"Over there are the vegetable gardens." Larmina pointed across the yard to raised beds full of spinach, tomatoes and other growing things. "They're on wheels so we can move them to get the most sun. We can grow a lot in small spaces. Parvana designed them."

Also out back were several sheds and smaller houses.

"That's where Parvana, Asif and Rafi live," Larmina said. "Next to that is where Zahra lives with her baby and Old Mrs. Musharef. Maryam's room is just behind theirs, on the other side of their wall. Oh, how Maryam complained about the baby waking her up in the morning! She wanted a house of her own. Parvana said no, that without a wake-up call, Maryam would sleep all day and there was no room in Green Valley for any laziness."

Larmina paused for a breath, then went on.

"I wonder who will get that room now. Probably Shauzia, since she can't go back to her barracks because of all the death threats against female police officers. She usually bunks with me and Hadiah when she stays here, but she'll likely want her own space if she's actually living here. She's fun to have around. Plus, she keeps the three sisters out of my hair sometimes, which gives me a bit of peace. They talk and talk and talk."

They passed back through the small gathering room where Damsa had napped, then into a kitchen with a long wooden table. Shauzia and some of the girls were making supper.

"Sometimes we do lessons here," Larmina said, tapping the table. "We eat in here or in the big room."

The big room was a much larger version of the small gathering room. Its bright walls were painted with flowers and geometric designs. There were toshaks along the walls, more cushions, a woodstove in the corner and a large cupboard at one end of the room.

"Parvana's office is over there, and our room is there, and there's a little supply cupboard in between. The younger girls sleep closer to the bathroom."

Damsa followed Larmina into a bedroom with six narrow cots.

"I'm here and Hadiah is over there. Sleep where you want except for those two beds. There used to be more girls here, older than me. One is now a journalist in Logar Province. She was always such a mess to live with, spread her stuff all over the room. I don't know how she can keep her facts straight now when she's doing her reporter job."

"I've never shared," said Damsa, looking around at the plain but cozy room with the handmade quilts folded neatly at the end of each cot. She compared it to the opulent bedroom she'd had at her father's house, with its heavy furniture, silk drapes and thick carpet.

"Who's that?" Damsa saw a framed photograph of an old woman hanging on the wall. The woman looked both fierce and kind at the same time. Beside the photo, also in a frame, was a gold medal on a bright ribbon.

"That's Mrs. Weera," Larmina said. "This was her property. She gave it to Parvana to build a women's center. There used to be women and children coming and going from here all day long. We had yoga classes, literacy, arithmetic lessons, classes on organizing a business, visiting nurses, visiting lawyers, a children's committee to improve the neighborhood, discussion groups on violence, politics, health, religion—everything. There was always something going on. It was so much fun! We put on plays and little concerts, Eid celebrations for the community, for anyone who wanted to come, men, too. Work, work, work, work, work, but that's fun, right?"

Damsa didn't have an answer. She had never worked a moment in her life. Anything that had needed doing, the servants had done.

Larmina sighed. "Then people got too afraid to come, and now it's pretty quiet here. We still do schoolwork, but it was more fun when there was a room full of people learning. Anyway, Mrs. Weera got the medal when she was younger for being the fastest woman runner in Afghanistan. She's gone now, heart attack, but there's a whole group of people called Friends of Mrs. Weera—women and men—who look out for girls like us. Anyone who needs help, really. I'm going to be one of them and do brave things. What are you going to do when you get older? It's all right. You don't have to answer. Right now, you want supper."

At supper, Damsa sat at the big table with chatter all around, everyone but her fetching and dishing out and keeping an eye on what the others needed. It was loud and happy, everyone talking and everyone listening and sharing their opinions.

Damsa remembered the silent meals at her old house, the servants slipping in with food, slipping out with empty platters. Her father would be preoccupied with business, often on his phone. Damsa's stepmother sometimes tried to ask everyone about their day and corrected Damsa's table manners. Damsa would keep her eyes on her plate, the heft of the expensive cutlery matching the heavy atmosphere.

It was so different here that Damsa wasn't sure how to behave. She felt shy to try. But everyone ignored her while at the same time passing her food and making sure she had enough to eat and drink. They included her in conversations through cheerful offhand comments like, "Now that Damsa's here, we can get some order in this place!"

The three sisters who had giggled while Damsa drooled sat across the table from her.

"Oldest to youngest, Alia, age ten, Noosala, nine, and Rosta, who's eight," said Larmina. "They all ran away together after Alia was whipped for refusing to marry."

"I found them in a town on the border with the next province, hiding in a bakery storage room," said Officer Shauzia. "They were covered in flour."

"Shauzia almost baked us in the oven," piped up little Rosta.

"Yes. I thought, how wonderful. Three delicious loaves of bread," said Shauzia, which got the three sisters giggling again.

Zahra sat beside Alia, with her child, Lara, in a

baby chair next to her on the table. Zahra giggled with the sisters. The baby held a piece of nan that she alternately chewed on or stared at in fascination.

Damsa tried not to stare at the young mother. That might have been her own fate, too, if she hadn't run out on her engagement. She could not imagine being responsible for a baby at her age.

Next to the baby, at the end of the table, Old Mrs. Musharef scooped up rice with her fingers.

"Call me old, that's right," she said to Damsa. "My husband tried to kill me, but I got away! I am old and alive, so being old is a victory. We have to celebrate our victories!"

At this, everyone applauded, and Damsa got the impression that clapping for each other was a routine thing here, the way they all did it, then went back to eating.

Parvana sat at the other end of the table, and beside her was a girl Damsa supposed was Hadiah. Hadiah had a book open beside her and read while she ate, joining in the clapping when it happened, otherwise perfectly content to concentrate on the words on the pages.

No one bothered her. They just let her read.

No one bothered Damsa, either. They didn't pester her with questions. They didn't stare. They let her eat. She felt welcome. She felt that they had already decided she was one of them.

It almost made her cry.

Later in the evening, Damsa was given a tray of tea things and asked to deliver it to Parvana and Shauzia out in the yard. She found them sitting at a small table in a little garden ringed by white-painted rocks.

"I'm supposed to bring you this," Damsa said. She held out the tray with tea, two cups and a small plate of biscuits.

"Welcome to France," said Shauzia.

That's when Damsa noticed the little sign with *France* painted on it.

"Yes, step into our lavender field." Parvana waved her hands at the two dozen or so tall feathery plants heavy with purple blossoms.

"That's not lavender," Damsa said. "That's Russian sage."

"Some call it Afghan lavender," said Shauzia. "Don't be shy. Join us."

Damsa put the tray down on the table.

"Have a seat."

A garden swing was near the table. Damsa sat and gently rocked back and forth. She spied a strange structure in the garden, a little taller than herself.

"What's that?"

"That's the Eiffel Tower," said Shauzia. "Parvana made it for me as a birthday present. Like the sign says, we're in France."

"Are you two all right?" Damsa asked.

"You'd better explain," said Parvana.

"When we were children, I carried a magazine picture of a lavender field in France," said Shauzia. "It looked like the most perfect place to be. My plan was to go there, sit in that field and no one would bother me ever again. I still might do that. But not today. Today is a good day. Parvana got a call from Asif. They've arrived at the safe house."

"I'll really feel better when Asif is back here and Nooria calls to say she's met Rafi at the airport in New York," Parvana said. "Then I'll be able to relax again."

"It's been a long haul, getting their trip together," said Shauzia. "Visas, paperwork, passports, tickets. All of it so complicated."

"And Maryam, who never makes anything easy." Parvana passed the plate of biscuits to Damsa. "Have a cookie."

Damsa took one. "Is Maryam really so difficult?"

"It's my own fault," said Parvana. "I didn't want her to have to be as serious as me, but she needed to be a little bit serious. Every time I tried to push her in that direction, she went all-in on irresponsibility."

"You liked that she was irresponsible," Shauzia said mildly. Clearly, the two of them had had this discussion before. "You said over and over that it was about time a woman in Afghanistan could finally act like there would always be enough for her—enough food, enough freedom and enough space. But between you and me, Damsa, Maryam is a lot tougher and kinder than she lets on. She'll be just fine." Shauzia took a swallow of tea and put her cup down. "Enough about her. How are you settling in?"

"I like it here," Damsa said. "I don't know how to do anything, though. We always had servants."

"It's more fun to be able to look after ourselves. You'll soon learn," said Parvana. "Try to relax and enjoy this place. No one will hurt you here or force you to do anything you don't want to do. You're with us now, for as long as you want. We take care of each other. Tell us about yourself. Did you go to school?"

"I was a good student," said Damsa, then hesitated. "Well, I got distracted a lot. Sometimes I studied. Sometimes I didn't."

"What did you enjoy studying?"

The two women looked like they were truly interested.

"The microscope," Damsa said. "Our school shared one with the boys' high school down the road. We didn't get a chance to use it very often, but my science teacher once let me look at slides through it for an entire lunch hour, all by myself."

"And what did you like about that?" asked Shauzia.

No one had ever asked Damsa questions like these. She had to think before she knew the answer.

"I liked that there are whole other worlds that we don't always see."

Shauzia and Parvana nodded.

Shauzia's cell phone rang. She answered it.

"Hello?...Really...Well, that was sooner than expected. Anything I can do?...Yes, I certainly will stay hidden, at least for now. You, too...Take care."

She hung up and put the phone on the table beside her cup of tea.

"That was one of my colleagues," she said. "A policewoman in the city. She called to tell me the news."

"What news?"

Damsa watched Shauzia take Parvana's hands in hers and hold them tight.

"The Taliban have taken Kabul. They've got the whole country now. They're back."

6

"I've never painted in the dark before," whispered Parvana.

"I've never painted at all," said Damsa. That was yet another item on a long list of things she had never done and had never even thought about doing, until today.

"I hope this is unnecessary," said Parvana. "Hadiah, if this was unnecessary, you have my deepest apology. Even if it turns out to be necessary, I am truly sorry."

"That's okay," said Hadiah. "I can always paint it again."

Those were the first words Damsa had heard Hadiah speak.

Damsa watched Parvana and Hadiah dip their wide brushes in the paint can and smooth away the drips. There was just enough moonlight to see the words "Green Valley" disappear under the paint.

"I can't tell what color this is," she whispered, as she mimicked their actions at the paint can.

"It's a very dull gray," said Parvana. "We'll start with the words to make sure we have enough paint, then work our way out to the flowers. We need to paint over the address numbers, too."

Damsa brushed a line of paint across some letters. Two of them vanished.

I'm painting, she thought with amazement. Her line dripped, but she smoothed out the drips with another stroke of the brush.

"If they have taken over Kabul, they have taken over the offices of the organizations that have helped us over the years," Parvana said. "We are very small now, but you should have seen us, Damsa, when we operated a full-service women's center. Those were busy times, right, Hadiah? The Taliban probably won't bother us now, Inshallah, but we need to do what we can to confuse them. If they can't find us..."

"They can't get us," finished Damsa.

There was enough moonlight to see Parvana's smile.

"I feel like I've been fighting the Taliban and people like them my whole life," said Parvana. "When the Taliban first came to power, I was living in Kabul with my family, all of us stuck in one room together — my father, my mother, my older sister, Nooria, Maryam, who was a very little girl, and our baby brother, Ali. It was hard before our father was arrested. After he was arrested, it was even worse."

Damsa wanted to ask why he'd been arrested, but she didn't want to be rude.

Parvana told her without her asking.

"He was educated in England. He taught history and literature and he loved stories. The Taliban thought he was an enemy. They kept him in prison for a long time. When they finally let him go, it was just him and me on the road. The rest of my family were in Mazar-e-Sharif. Then he died, and it was just me."

"Is that when you met Shauzia? Larmina told me you were girls together."

"Boys together is more like it," said Parvana with a little laugh. "I knew Shauzia from school, but we really got to know each other after my father was arrested. We turned ourselves into boys in order to move freely on the streets and find work. Our families depended on us."

"That's incredible," said Damsa.

"Poor Hadiah has heard this story too many times," said Parvana. "But, yes, Shauzia and I go way back. Mrs. Weera, too. She was our gym teacher when we were little girls in school. When the Taliban came, she led women working in secret and then later she was elected to Parliament. So the lesson, dear Damsa, is that where we think we are going when we start out our journey is often not where we end up."

Damsa painted some more. She liked the feeling of spreading paint, even though they were covering up something beautiful with a color that was not.

Safety is beautiful, though, she thought, and then she was surprised that her brain, something that had never felt like much use to her, could produce a thought that profound.

She wondered what else she could do.

They worked quickly. The flowers disappeared under the gray, and soon the beautiful, bright, special gate was dull and anonymous.

Green Valley was down a little lane all its own. Outside its walls, a pathway to the right led to a thicket of trees and small plots of cultivated land, growing vegetables and fodder for sheep and goats. The path to the left led to a collection of three-story shells of apartment buildings, which either had been bombed or not quite completed.

They were far away from other homes, but it still seemed like a good idea to be quiet.

"There's a little village that way," Parvana said, when she saw Damsa looking at the uncompleted buildings. "There are some shops, some houses. When we get the chance, I'll take you for a walk so you'll know how to get around."

"In case you have to escape," said Hadiah.

"That's right," said Parvana. "It's important to know your options."

"I already escaped," said Damsa. She had been thirsty, hungry and so, so scared. "I didn't like it."

"But it brought you here," said Parvana. "You took a chance and now you are making a whole new life for yourself." She stood back. "I think we are done with this gate. We've got some paint left. As soon as it gets light in the morning I'll come back out and touch up any spots we've missed."

Parvana opened the door in the gate and put the paint can and the gray-covered brushes inside. She came back out with a small pot of white paint and another brush. With deft strokes, she painted over the address markings.

"You girls go inside. I'll just zip down the lane and paint over the sign that's posted there."

"Buddy system," said Hadiah. "I'll come with you."

They started walking. Damsa tagged along with them.

"Buddy system?" she asked.

"No one goes out alone," said Parvana. "That way, if anything happens, there is someone to run for help."

Damsa felt so, so good, walking down the dark lane with a purpose and with people who seemed to like her. It was a new experience.

At the end of the lane, Parvana flattened herself against the wall of the mechanic's shop. Damsa and Hadiah did the same.

Parvana peered around the corner. There was more light in front, from a naked bulb over the shop door. It made their darkness seem darker.

"We're clear," Parvana whispered. She opened the paint, handed the lid to Damsa, then quickly painted over the small sign that read *Green Valley* with an arrow pointing up the lane.

"Hadiah, think of something I can write on here in the morning when the paint is dry," said Parvana.

"How about *Oranges*, with the arrow going the other way?" Hadiah suggested.

"That's nice and confusing," agreed Parvana. She took the lid back from Damsa, and they hurried back up the lane.

By the time they saw the Talib waiting for them in the dark, it was too late to run away.

7

He was big. His gun and his turban made him bigger.

Parvana stopped. She silently bent down and put the can of paint and the brush in a clump of weeds, then stood tall and took a strong grip on Damsa and Hadiah, one girl in each hand. She walked them toward the Talib.

"Salaam alaikum," she said, bobbing her head in greeting.

She kept them walking, almost right up to the man with the gun. Then she turned them onto the pathway going to the left, toward the shells of buildings.

"It is unusual for you to be out so late," said the Talib.

"These are unusual times," replied Parvana. Weeds slapped Damsa's trembling legs with each step she took along the narrow path.

"We bid you good night," said Parvana. "We must get home."

"Parvana." The Talib spoke the word quietly and without a question mark.

Parvana kept herself and the girls moving. Damsa stayed close.

"You were my teacher."

They kept walking.

"*'O beauty, I asked, what makes you cry?*
Life is too short for me, it answered.'"

The Talib continued, "That is by Nazo Tokhi. She was born in Kandahar in 1651 and died in 1717."

Parvana turned around then. She pushed Damsa and Hadiah behind her, guarding them with her body.

"I remember you," she said. "You attended our adult women's literacy classes, slipping in so quiet and well behaved it took us months to realize you weren't attached to any of the women there. Even as a boy, you were drawn to the ancient poets. Your name is Gulam. Am I remembering right?"

"You remember," said Gulam, the Talib. "The poetry I learned here is just as you said, an umbrella in the rain, a blanket in the snow, sunshine on a dark day, and a companion in my despair. Thank you."

"But now you are with them." Parvana's words were not an accusation, just a statement.

"Take your own lessons, teacher," said Gulam. "You told us we are all individuals. If I joined the Taliban, it is because the corruption and the ruin that is Afghanistan pushed me into it. Where else could I go to have a life?"

"We *are* all individuals," said Parvana, her voice stronger now. She took steps forward. Damsa and

Hadiah stayed behind Parvana's back. "You are an individual who loves poetry and has joined an organization that burns books and closes schools. Why are you here?"

The Talib stepped to one side.

Two small children quivered in a clump, clinging to one another so tightly that they looked like one girl with two heads.

"I found them beside their dead grandfather," he said. "They have no one. They are better off with you than anywhere else."

Parvana knelt down in front of the children. Their whimpering sounded to Damsa like the mewing of kittens.

"If I take them in, get them fed and cleaned up," said Parvana, looking at the children but speaking to Gulam, "how do I know that you and your brother Talibs won't be back, wanting them for wives? If that is your plan, be merciful. Kill them now instead of subjecting them to a life of pain and servitude and abuse."

"It does not matter what I say," said the Talib. "You will not turn these children away. It is not in you to do that."

"How do you know?"

"Because you did not turn me away when I was a child, every bit as filthy and hungry and unlovable as these."

"They are not unlovable," said Parvana, her voice softening, "and neither were you. But what was the point of all that care if you have just gone and joined the enemy of life and beauty?"

"The point is that you helped me become the sort of man who would bring these girls to you instead of selling them to the highest bidder. Teacher," he said with respect. "I cannot guarantee that more Taliban won't come to your door. I follow orders. I don't make them. But I can promise that when I walk away tonight, whether you take the children or not, I will forget this place exists."

Parvana was silent a moment. Then she said, "Of course I'll take the children."

She nodded toward Damsa and Hadiah, who came forward and guided the two little ones through the door in the gate. They closed the door and stood behind the gate, listening.

"Here is some food," said the Talib. Damsa heard the rustle of a bag being exchanged. "You fed me, now I help you feed them. I hope that is enough to save my soul."

"Your soul is always in your hands," said Parvana. "Even as a member of the Taliban, you have choices to make."

"And my choice tonight is to forget," said Talib Gulam. "I will not remember you or Green Valley. I will not remember anything."

Damsa heard his feet on the gravel as he stepped away. She almost missed his last words.

"Except for poetry. I will remember poetry."

A moment later, Parvana came through the door. She had fetched the pot of white paint and the brush from the weeds.

She looked down at the two little girls, then she looked at Damsa and Hadiah.

"Always more tea to make, always more tears to dry," she said. "Baths, bread, bed."

They led the little ones down the dark stone pathway and into the warmth and soft light that was Green Valley.

8

❝ Why aren't we moving?" Maryam asked for the tenth time.

The car was completely stopped.

"We should have left earlier," said Asif.

"I don't see why we had to leave as early as we did," said Maryam. "We'll have to sit at our gate for hours with nothing to do."

"Maybe you could give a concert," Rafi said. His tone was not respectful. His father put a hand on his arm and frowned when Rafi turned to look at him.

"Sorry," Rafi said, so quietly it would have been louder if he had whispered.

His father squeezed his hand and smiled. "This will be a great story for you to tell your grandchildren, yes? *Escape from Kabul*. You could turn it into a ballet."

"No one wants to see a ballet about Afghanistan," Rafi said. "They want to see *The Nutcracker*. They want to see *Swan Lake*."

"What about a ballet called *Swans of Afghanistan*?" Asif suggested. "We grow almonds in Afghanistan.

What about *The Almond Sheller* instead of *The Nutcracker*?"

They were such awful suggestions that Rafi immediately felt better. If his father was calm enough to come up with bad ideas, he must not be too worried about getting to the airport.

Rafi couldn't believe the crush of cars and people. It looked like all of Afghanistan was trying to get to the airport. Everywhere they turned, they were met by crowds carrying bundles and vehicles full of people.

The car rolled slowly forward. Little by little, they made progress.

"It's a checkpoint," Asif said. "Everyone stay calm. Maryam, stay silent."

The waiting was awful. Rafi felt like he couldn't breathe. He could hear his heart thumping in his chest as if he'd been leaping around the yard for an hour.

"Rafi," his father said calmly, "what would your mother tell you to do right now?"

"Multiplication," Rafi answered without thinking. He'd heard the stories so many times. Reciting multiplication tables to herself had kept his mother calm when she was young and in danger.

Rafi didn't recite a times table. He recited the ballet positions he had learned on the internet.

"Pas de chat. Pirouette. Arabesque. Battement. Cabriole."

"Salaam alaikum."

A member of the Taliban stuck his head through the car window beside Rafi's father.

"Walaikum asalaam," replied Asif.

Another Talib knocked on the window by Rafi. Rafi rolled down the window. He smiled at the Talib.

"Salaam alaikum," Rafi said in greeting.

"Polite boy," said the Talib.

"He's a good son," said Asif.

"Who's that?" The Talib nodded at the silent Maryam, hidden in the burqa.

"My wife's sister," Asif said. "We are taking her to her new husband."

"Where is your wife?"

"Home. Where she belongs."

"Where they all belong, eh, brother?"

"Inshallah," said Asif.

"Stay away from the airport," the Talib advised. "Go around. The foreigners are all running away and they're clogging up the streets."

Asif said thank you, and they were waved on.

"You'd better get me on that plane," Maryam said from the back seat.

"I want that just as much as you do," said Asif.

He turned down a side street. Rafi saw a Talib swinging a stick at a small group of uncovered women. The women were fast. They got away.

"Papa?" he asked in a panic.

"We need to keep calm," his father said.

"All right," said Rafi. *Pas de chat. Pirouette. Arabesque* ...

Asif turned down one street and then another, looking for a clear way to the airport.

All the shops were shuttered. There were many Taliban soldiers strutting around together on foot or riding around in pickup trucks. Rafi saw their white flags flying from shop fronts and rooftops. He saw guns, guns and more guns held aloft, pointed at people, slung over shoulders and shooting rapidly into the air in celebration.

"Papa?" he asked again.

"We'll get there," his father said.

But they couldn't even get close.

Every time they tried, their way was blocked by crowds, by cars and by Taliban checkpoints.

Rafi checked their plane tickets again. Their flight left in three hours.

"We're not that far from the airport," Asif said. "Perhaps we should leave the car and walk."

"What? No!" Maryam said. "I can't carry all that luggage. All my things. My concert dresses. No. We're not leaving the car."

"I know you're scared," Asif said in a soothing voice. "We will stick together and get you through the airport doors. Then I'll come back to the car with a cart and a porter and we will get the rest of your luggage. That would work, wouldn't it?"

Rafi looked at his father with alarm. Asif could not possibly manage the crowd and all that luggage by himself.

"I'll go back with you," he said.

"You will put your listening ears on," Asif said. "Did you not hear me say that I will come back to the car with a porter and a cart? You will stay with your aunt, just inside the door of the airport, where I can easily find you when I return. I will give you a deadline. If I am not back by that deadline, you will take your aunt through security and get on the plane."

"Without my things?" asked Aunt Maryam.

"You are free to stay here in Afghanistan with your things if you want," replied Asif, again in that mild tone.

"What if she won't go with me?" Rafi asked.

"Then you will hand over her ticket and her papers and continue on by yourself. I'm not getting into trouble with your mother on this. Remember, Rafi. Your main job is to get yourself on the plane."

Asif drove around some more, hoping to get close, to find a place where the crowds were thinnest. He finally maneuvered the car into an alley and turned off the engine.

"One small bag each," Asif ordered. "Take only what you can carry easily. Rafi, check for your documents."

Rafi had a pouch around his neck, hidden under his clothes. It had been specially sewn by Parvana, big enough for the tickets, passports, visas and contact information, plus enough American cash to get them to Nooria's apartment in case she failed to meet them at the other end.

After only a little bit of whining, which told Rafi his aunt was too scared to properly complain, Maryam got out of the car, gripping her carry-on luggage, a small suitcase on wheels. She had her purse slung across her shoulders under her burqa. Asif carried her backpack for her.

Rafi put his grandfather's shoulder bag over his head so that the strap crossed his body, with no chance of slipping off. Over that, he put on his backpack, the one he'd used for school, and he was ready.

"Don't bother about my suitcase, Papa," he said. "I have everything I really need right on me. I can live my whole life out of these two bags."

"My wandering Afghan," his father said. Then he turned to Maryam. "Are you ready?"

"Don't lose me," Maryam said.

Rafi gripped her hand. "Don't let go." He put his other hand on his father's arm. Asif adjusted his crutches, and they started walking toward the airport.

9

❝ It's a swing."

Damsa moved the swinging chair gently back and forth. The two little girls eyed it with suspicion.

They'd been washed and now wore the clean clothes Larmina had found for them in the supply cupboard. The clothes were only a little bit too big for them. Their hair was brushed out of their eyes and tied with blue ribbons. They'd had a small meal before bed and a bigger breakfast that morning with eggs and milk.

Now they were in *Leila's Playground*, according to the brightly painted sign, and Damsa was in charge of them.

She had never been in charge of anything in her life.

The way it happened didn't exactly boost her confidence much, though.

"Do you know how to work in a vegetable garden?" Larmina asked. "Cook? Sew?" The list of what she had to admit to the other girl that she did not know how to do grew with every suggestion Larmina made.

"Better take the new kids out to play," Larmina finally suggested. "Even if all they do is sit together and watch you, they're out in the sun and they're learning."

Damsa wondered who made Larmina the boss of her. Weren't they all supposed to be queens? But everyone else was busy with chores, so Damsa wanted to contribute, too.

Damsa lifted the littlest one onto the bench in the playground and the other one climbed up beside her.

"Watch me," Damsa said. "I'm going to show you how to play on all these things, and if you want to play, too, well, that would be just fine."

The little girls didn't say anything. Neither of them had spoken a word since they arrived. They huddled together on the bench, not a millimeter of space between them, and they kept their eyes on Damsa.

"This is how we use the swing." Damsa sat on the swing and used her legs to gently sway back and forth. "It's really fun. You can go high if you want but you don't have to. Would you like to try?"

No response, but she got the feeling they were paying attention, so she kept on swinging.

Who am I? she thought.

She barely recognized herself. In a very short time, she had gone from being a girl who demanded—and got—the best of everything and never lifted a finger to help anyone, to a girl who wore second-or-maybe-third-or-even-fourth-hand clothes, who had painted a gate in the middle of the night. A girl who had just had the best sleep of her life, on a narrow bunk in a room she shared with girls she hardly knew.

I'm a girl on an adventure, she decided.

She liked that idea. An adventurer was someone who was brave, who went out into the unknown even if she was scared, who wanted new and exciting, not just old and comfortable.

The smallest girl was already asleep, leaning against her sister. Damsa wondered if she should wake the child up. She really knew nothing about small children. She had never been around them.

"She's going to fall right off that bench."

Old Mrs. Musharef walked into the playground carrying baby Lara. In a smooth, unhurried motion, she handed the baby to Damsa, picked up the sleeping newcomer and sat on the bench with the young one in her lap.

To the other girl, she said, "Go on, play. Nothing here is going to bite you." To Damsa, she said, "I can take Lara, too. Plenty of room on my lap."

Damsa was happy to hand over the baby. She'd never held a baby before and wasn't comfortable doing it now.

The little girl climbed the steps to the slide. Damsa felt both unwanted and unneeded. She left them to it and walked away from the playground.

Maybe she would see how their paint job looked in the daylight. Parvana had said she would check at dawn to see if it needed touch-ups, and to put a new fake address on the gatepost. If she had forgotten, Damsa could do it, and then everyone would know she was useful.

She opened the door in the gate and looked out. The gate needed no touch-ups, and the new address was already there.

"Going somewhere?"

Officer Shauzia was right behind her.

"No, I'm just—"

"You can leave any time you want," said Shauzia, "but please tell us first. We can help you get where you want to go, or at least give you the best chance of getting there safely. Certainly no guarantee these days."

"I wasn't going anywhere!"

"Then please don't stand around the open door, advertising that you're here. We never know who is watching."

"Nobody is out there."

"You don't know that." Shauzia closed the door and bolted it shut. "We all need to be very careful."

And then she just walked away, leaving Damsa alone by the closed gate.

I should leave, Damsa thought.

But she had no intention of leaving. She had been out in the world on her own for just a few days, but it was enough for her to know that she never wanted to do that again. Being hungry, thirsty, filthy and exhausted was awful, but the worst was not knowing if a stranger's glance was out of curiosity or because they had been sent by her father to kill her. It had felt like there was danger everywhere.

She could go to the kitchen and try to help. There must be something in there she could learn to do. Same with the vegetable gardens, and there were probably more clothes that needed to be scrubbed.

But she was sure that whatever she tried, there would be someone close by who could do it better.

What she really wanted was to just get away—but not too far away.

She wandered around the compound, looking for a place where she could be by herself.

At the back of the compound were several sheds and smaller buildings. Three contained living quarters. She looked in their windows but didn't go in. One room was fancier than the others, with big mirrors. She guessed that had been where Maryam slept.

There was another shed off in a corner. The door was open. No one was inside, so she stepped in.

Her eyes got used to the dim.

The shed was full of toys.

There were toy trucks, toy buses, toy houses and toy schools. There were toys made from wood, toys made from metal, toys made from leather and toys that were made from a combination of all three.

Tools hung neatly from hooks and nails on the wall. Shelves held pieces of leather and boxes of nails.

Damsa saw several small engines and metal pieces that looked like they might belong in engines. Old military-looking bits of metal were piled in a corner.

"He can fix anything."

Damsa spun around. Parvana was watching her from the doorway.

"Asif is a gifted mechanic," Parvana continued. "He makes toys for fun. He makes them from things that are thrown away, mostly old war junk. Turns something that kills children into something that makes them smile."

Parvana picked up a toy bus and spun one of its wheels absentmindedly.

"War took his leg when he was little," she said. "Did anyone tell you yet that we met in a cave? We were both children, younger than you. He was alone. I was traveling with a baby I'd found in a bombed-out house. Hassan. That baby is now an ambulance driver in Herat. Makes me feel old."

Parvana picked up the toy on Asif's workbench—a bear made of wood and metal with arms and legs that moved. It was waiting for a coat of paint.

"Asif and I did not like each other! We drove each other around the bend. We argued our way across Afghanistan. He'd get me so mad, I forgot I was hungry. He'd get me so mad, I forgot I was scared! But we kept that baby and each other alive."

She put the bear back on the workbench.

"And now he's aggravating me again because he has not called to tell me everything is all right. What about you, Damsa? Are you taking a break from everyone?"

"Everybody here knows how to do things," Damsa told her. "I got tired of not knowing."

"Fair enough," said Parvana. "Nobody is born knowing things, though. You'll learn as you go."

Damsa looked at the shelves. "Do you think Asif would teach me how to make toys?"

"He'll teach you to use all the tools, whether you're interested or not! You'll learn basic auto mechanics, how to use a screwdriver, how to hang a door. He teaches everyone these things. You'll learn first aid, too. Everyone does. You're clever. You'll catch on fast."

"You think I'm clever? I've never felt clever. My teachers all said my mind wandered too much to do me any good."

"Your mind could focus on the microscope," Parvana pointed out. "If you give it a chance, you'll be surprised at what else it could do."

Damsa had just started to think about that when Shauzia's voice reached them.

"Parvana! Parvana, where are you? You're never where you should be."

"In here!" Parvana left the shed. "Did you hear anything? Did he call?"

Shauzia's long strides brought her to them.

"He called," she said. "His phone is low on battery. They're still in Kabul. They didn't get on the plane. There are no more commercial flights. The airport has been shut down."

10

"Papa, you need to sit."

The crowd wasn't so thick now. Word must have spread that the airport was closed. Rafi was able to guide his father to a patch of grass. He made sure Maryam was following them. He helped his father lower himself to the ground. Maryam flipped back her burqa and she sat, too.

"Call Parvana again," Maryam said. "Tell her to figure out another flight for us."

"My phone doesn't have much battery left," said Asif. "Let's see if we can learn something new first."

Rafi opened his grandfather's shoulder bag and got each of them a bit of nan and a few almonds. They chewed and swallowed and each had a drink of water from one of the bottles in the bag. Rafi knew there was more food and water in the backpacks but he didn't know how long it would have to last.

"Papa, if you stay here with Aunt Maryam, I'll go and see what I can find out."

"We should stay together," said Asif.

"I know," said Rafi, getting to his feet. "I won't go far. Stay right here." He looked up. They were sitting below a billboard. A smiling child ate a cracker next to a giant blue-and-white box. "I won't be long."

Rafi left them there.

I didn't ask permission, he thought.

If he'd asked, he would have been told no. That's why he had to get away before his father could tell him not to go.

Rafi felt very grown-up, walking around on his own. At home his mother kept a pretty tight rein on him. He *could* go out on his own to school or to football, or to his friend's house—before his friend went away to Germany—but he hardly ever got the chance. Almost always, there was Parvana or Maryam or Larmina or Old Mrs. Musharef around, eager for a trip to the village. The rule about the buddy system was pretty strict. Rafi rarely went out alone.

Today, even though he was in a big crowd, even though he was scared and had people he loved depending on him to do this very important task, he felt a spark of joy inside him. Today he was not a small boy being told what to do.

He was a man, finding help for others.

He went up to one of the American soldiers guarding the airport gate.

"Good afternoon," Rafi said in perfect English. All the children under his mother's care learned to speak basic phrases in several languages. Rafi, the grandson of an English teacher and the son of a woman who was fluent in English, spoke English himself almost as well as he spoke Dari and Pashtu.

He dug into his grandfather's shoulder bag and brought out a bag of nuts and dried fruit. He offered it to the soldier.

"Would you like a snack?" he asked. "It's hard work, guarding this gate."

The soldier had been looking in several directions at once, answering questions, telling people to stand back and be patient. Rafi's young, clear voice broke through the confusion.

She motioned to her brother soldiers to keep an eye out. Then she knelt down by Rafi.

"That's kind of you to offer," the soldier said. "But no, thank you."

Rafi put the snack away. He saw a wildflower that miraculously had not been trampled on and bent down and picked it. He held it out to the soldier.

"To remind you that Afghanistan is beautiful," he said.

The soldier smiled. She had green eyes that smiled with her.

"Afghanistan is the most beautiful place on earth," she said. "Do you know why?"

"Why?"

"Because the people are so kind."

She took the flower.

Rafi heard the click of a camera. He looked up to see someone with PRESS on their shirt taking his picture.

"What's your name, son?" the PRESS guy asked.

"Rafi. What's your name?"

"Kwami. Are you with your parents?"

"My father is over by the billboard. He's tired. He only has one leg."

The reporter left them.

Rafi leaned closer to the soldier so that the people around them would not know his business.

"My aunt and I have visas for the United States and airplane tickets," Rafi said. "Will you let us into the airport, please?"

The soldier said quietly, "There will be a general announcement soon, but I'll tell you now so you can get a head start. Your father will need the extra time. There are no more civilian flights. We're waiting for more soldiers to arrive so that we can reopen the airport safely. People with the right documents will be airlifted on military planes. Do you know where the military side of the airport is?"

Rafi shook his head.

"I'm not going to point because I don't want to start a rush, but turn to your left and keep walking around the perimeter. You'll come to it. There are several gates. I don't know which gate will open or when."

Rafi thanked her, then stepped back into the crowd.

"What did you say? What did she say?"

"She said Afghanistan is a beautiful country," he said and kept walking. He had to get back to his father and his aunt and get them to the military gate before a stampede of people blocked their way.

He felt he was swimming against a river as he pushed against people who were pushing at him, trying to get to the gate. When he finally broke free, he was far from where he thought he was.

Fortunately, the billboard was like a beacon, and he made it back to his father and Maryam.

"We have to get to the military airport," he told them quietly. "There won't be any more flights from this airport. They are taking people with documents out on military planes."

"How do you know someone from the *New York Times*?" his father asked. "I gave him permission to use your picture."

"He can't be a very good reporter," said Aunt Maryam. "He'd never heard of me."

Rafi rolled his eyes.

"Can you walk now or do you need more rest?" he asked his father.

"Can't we drive?" Maryam asked.

Rafi and his father ignored her question. Rafi strapped on his backpack, helped his father stand, and then they waited while Maryam got herself together.

"Take Rafi's hand," Asif told her. "If you lose us, you'll be impossible to find."

"Why don't I just take this cover off?" Maryam asked, shaking the burqa in frustration.

"If you are recognized, people might think you have the power to get them on a plane because you are famous," said Asif. "They could swamp you and put you in danger."

"My fans do love me," Maryam said. She kept the burqa on.

Rafi took Aunt Maryam's hand, and the three of them headed toward the military side of the airport.

They could not move fast. Clumps of people crossed their path, going this way or that, so they could not take more than a few steps before waiting for someone to pass. There were people lying on the ground, too, resting, or — Rafi feared — dead from the heat or exhaustion. His father had a hard time maneuvering through all this, and Maryam found new things to complain about with every step. It made the walk long and it made Rafi irritated.

"Where are you going?"

Taliban soldiers blocked their way.

"My son and sister-in-law are going to the airport," Asif said.

Rafi could tell from the tone in his voice how very tired his father was.

"Why do they want to go there?"

"They are going to live with my wife's sister in America."

"America?" repeated the Talib. "They want to leave Afghanistan? You're sending your son to the other side of the world when he should be staying to build his country. I'm not sending *my* son to America. What kind of a father are you?"

"We both want what's best for our children," Asif said.

"What's best is to stay, not run away."

"Please let us pass."

"No," said the Talib. "You need to think about this some more. Go and think. You'll see that I am right. You think your life will be good in America, young man? It won't be. They don't want you there. I know. I was there for three years, in cooking school. Mean people, the Americans. Insulting people. Go. Sit. Reconsider."

Asif turned Rafi and Maryam around. He led them down an alley, then turned down a street that ran parallel to the airport. They kept walking.

They walked and walked. It seemed like they were walking around the whole airport, always through crowds, always trying to keep the airport fence in sight. They had to stop and sit when Rafi could tell that his father could not take another step, but they rested only minutes. Maryam was so tired, she stopped complaining.

They made it to the North Gate on the military side. It was closed and blocked by soldiers. Rafi got his father and aunt settled on another patch of grass, then went to talk to the soldiers.

"Go back to your homes," the soldiers kept repeating to all the people gathered around them. "This gate is closed for the rest of the day. Go back to your homes."

The soldiers took no notice of Rafi, no matter how perfect his English.

He went back to Asif and Maryam. Maryam's burqa was raised. She was breathing in great gulps of air.

It wasn't exactly fresh air. It was air that smelled of exhaust fumes, human waste and unwashed bodies. It was air filled with the stink of an open sewer ditch not far from where they sat and not far from the airport fence.

Rafi passed a bottle of water to his aunt.

"Don't drink too much," he said. "We don't know how long it has to last."

To his surprise, Maryam did not argue. She took two swallows, then passed the bottle to Asif. He drank and passed it back to Rafi.

The water was warm in Rafi's throat. It did not refresh him.

He watched the crowd. People walked in all directions. Someone got what they thought was a hot tip, hurried off, and crowds followed, thinking that a gate was opening somewhere. There were families in Western clothes, families in traditional clothes and families wearing combinations of both. There were old people stooped over walking sticks, young people with phones out and suitcases on wheels, people carrying children and children carrying babies. Others sat on the ground like Rafi and his family, eating snacks they'd brought with them or just gathering their energy for whatever would come next.

They all wanted to get out of Afghanistan.

A man with a tired face sat nearby with two toddlers. He leaned against a large suitcase, his head slumped down and his beard touching his chest. One of the toddlers watched an ant crawl across her hand. The other child put her own hand up to her sister's and the ant traveled back and forth between the girls. They giggled as its legs tickled their skin.

Their father woke with a start and looked angry about the noise the children were making. Then Rafi watched his face soften as he leaned in to help them count the legs on the ant.

Rafi raised his eyes and watched military planes circle, their bellies low as they approached the runway with a monstrous roar.

Beside him, his father and aunt slept on the grass.

He stayed awake, and kept them safe.

11

Rafi, Asif and Maryam spent the night on that patch of grass.

The crowds around them kept growing. Asif was afraid that if they moved, they would be shoved farther back. Rafi was glad they had the extra food his mother had packed. He also felt that if he had all the water in the world, it would not be enough to stop his thirst.

The ground was hard and rocky, but at least they had the comfort of knowing they were at the airport, close to the place that could take them to a new life. It was just on the other side of the fence. So very close.

"Today we go to the gate," his father whispered when the morning was still dark. "We will stand right at the front of the line, and we will stay there until they let us through."

Rafi gently woke his aunt.

Silently, they got to their feet. Rafi strapped on his grandfather's shoulder bag, and they inched their way through the sleeping bodies.

They got to the edge of the gully and stopped.

The gate was half a football field away to their left. To get there on solid ground, they would have to walk through people who were tightly packed in next to one another. Asif would never make it through on his crutches. They would surely step on someone. The commotion that would come next would wake everyone up and cause a crush at the gate, leaving Rafi and his family far behind.

The only other way to get there was to wade through the little river of raw sewage that flowed through the gully.

Maryam, her burqa flipped back so she could see, hesitated, but Rafi was more concerned for his father. Maryam was squeamish, but she had two strong legs. His father had one, and he was not as healthy as he should have been for a man his age.

Rafi went first.

Down the little hill and right into the filthy, stinking water. It was cold and disgusting and came up to his belly.

"Take the phone," Asif said, handing the cell phone to Maryam. "You are less likely to fall in the water than I am."

Maryam put the cell phone in her purse and closed the clasp. She put a knot in the strap so that the purse hung down to her armpit rather than to her waist. It would be safer from the water that way.

Rafi motioned to Maryam to follow him. She shook her head. She kept shaking it, even as she took a step forward in her little black shoes. She bit her lip as the water touched her skin. Rafi could see the tears running down her cheeks, but she did not cry out. He was proud of her.

He and Maryam helped his father into the gully.

Slowly, with each slosh of their legs, the gate got closer.

"I forgot my suitcase!" Maryam said suddenly. "My carry-on bag! And we don't have the backpacks!"

"I have all we need," Rafi said. "The visas and the passports." They kept going, step by terrible step.

There was no way he was going to try to turn around now, and he doubted the press of people behind them would let them go back. Even though it was very early, others were already in the gully ahead of them, and even more were behind.

Somewhere in the crowd, a baby cried.

That was all it took to wake everyone up. Within minutes, the area in front of the gate was alive with surging bodies as people tried to get closer to the gate and were pushed back by those who were ahead of them, trying to protect their positions.

Finally, Rafi and his father and aunt could go no farther. The people in front of them in the gully were a solid wall. The people behind them were another wall.

They were stuck in the gully, up to their bellies in other people's waste.

Everyone stood pressed in together, eyes on the gate, and waited.

The morning turned from gray to bright as the sun rose and the heat rose with it. The stench rose with the heat. Rafi watched a man faint and slip down into the foul water. People around him pulled him out and laid him on the gully bank, half in and half out of the water. Rafi couldn't tell if the man was still alive.

"Papa?" he asked. "Are you okay? You can sit."

The only way his father could sit was if he left the gully.

"You should go home now," Rafi told his father. "Mama is going to be worried. I'll get us on the plane. You don't need to be here."

Asif straightened the cap on Rafi's head.

"Your mother will have my head if I go home without a signed letter from the pilot saying that you are on the plane," he joked. "It does her good to worry. Reminds her how much she loves us."

"I dare you to tell her that," said Maryam, and they all laughed, even though it wasn't that funny.

Rafi passed around a bottle of water, and they ate some nuts and dried apricots, even though eating and drinking while standing in sewer water was nauseating.

"Give us water," a young man asked. "You have water. We have none. You have to share."

"We have very little," Asif said.

"You're not going to share? Give it to us! Give us water!"

"Who has water?" Rafi heard. "Are they giving out water?"

The wave of humans rolled as the rumors of water or any kind of help went through the crowd. Asif took advantage of the shifting crowd and pulled Rafi and Maryam ten meters closer to the gate.

A military truck drove up to the airport side of the gate and everyone forgot about water.

American soldiers got out of the truck and stood behind the wire gate. One of them took out a bullhorn.

"Listen to us," the soldier said. "Everyone, quiet, and listen to me."

The crowd went quiet. The American handed the bullhorn to an Afghan interpreter.

"If you have a visa to enter the United States, take it out so we can see it," the interpreter shouted. "Only people with the correct papers are being allowed into the airport today. If you have the correct papers, hold them up."

The gate was unlocked then. A phalanx of soldiers kept the crowd from flooding inside.

Rafi and his family got pushed along by the crowd. People were getting through the gate! They were getting inside the airport grounds!

"Take the papers out," ordered Maryam. "Take them out. You heard what he said!"

"When we get closer," said Rafi. "I don't want to drop them in the water."

Just ahead of them, that's exactly what happened. A man held three American passports high in the air. He was jostled, and they slipped through his fingers, dropping into the muck. He called for help to find them, but everyone was too concerned for themselves.

Rafi managed to scoop up one of the passports, but when he held it out, dripping, to the man, the man was too upset to thank him.

"One passport? What am I supposed to do with one passport? There are three of us!"

"Rafi!" said his father.

Rafi looked at Asif.

"You and Maryam go on up there. We will say goodbye now."

He grabbed Rafi in a tight embrace.

"Call us from New York," he said. "Become a great dancer. You are already a great man."

Asif pushed him away.

"Go!"

The crowd gave Rafi no chance to argue. It pushed him and Maryam closer to the gate, away from his father, away from the man who loved him more than any other man ever would, and there was nothing Rafi could do but keep going forward.

The gate was within reach now. All they would have to do was crawl up the bank of the gully, out of the sewer water, and up to the soldiers.

Rafi stuck his hand under his collar, ready to pull up the pouch that contained their papers, their passports to a better, safer life. His other hand was so completely fused to his Aunt Maryam's hand it was like they were welded together.

Two more steps, and they were at the edge of the water. Three big steps, and they were out of the gully. A dozen more steps on dry land, and they would be at the gate, and then through it.

And that's when the explosion happened.

12

It was noise and it was blood and it was bodies.

It was dust and chunks of concrete and a roar from the devil.

Rafi hid his face in the folds of his aunt's burqa, and Maryam protected his head with her arms.

They stayed like that a long, long time.

Then the wailing began.

Rafi unfolded himself. He was covered in dust and debris that fell off him as he moved his arms. Aunt Maryam was also covered in dust and muck, but she was still there, she was still alive and with him.

"Papa!" he yelled. His cry was lost in a symphony of other cries, as survivors combed among the wounded and the dead for the people they loved.

He saw the bodies of American soldiers. He saw the bodies of Afghans on the grass, on the bank of the gully, and floating in the fetid water.

Rafi stumbled to his feet.

I can still walk, he thought. *My legs aren't hurt. I can still dance.*

And then his head cleared, and he hated himself for having such a selfish thought.

"Stay here," he ordered Maryam. "Do not move. If you move, I won't be able to find you again. I have to find my father." He made himself sound like his mother. "Do not move. Do you understand?"

Maryam nodded. "I'll stay. But come back!"

Rafi stepped among severed arms and someone's intestines, slipping on blood and sewage. He helped a girl out of the gully. He lifted a baby off the ground and held it high in the air as it screamed, until a woman, screaming just as frantically as the baby, grabbed it from Rafi's hands and held it close, then ran off.

Rafi looked all around.

"Papa!" he called out, one voice of many calling for their fathers or mothers or children. "Papa!"

Asif could not have gone far. The explosion happened soon after he'd said goodbye. His father moved slowly on a good day, and the crowds would have made his progress even slower.

Rafi looked back at the gully he'd just crawled out of. He measured with his eyes where he had been when his father said goodbye. He tried to calculate how far Asif could have gotten.

He watched men pull bodies from the gully. He watched and saw that one of those bodies was still alive! The man gasped for air as he was lifted up and gently set down on the gravel.

Rafi plunged back into the water.

"Papa!" he called out again and again, plunging his hands into the little river and pulling up whatever he managed to grasp—a severed leg, a piece of luggage, a woman's purse, a dead baby that was quickly taken from him by adult hands, hands that would know what to do, if something was to be done.

Then, just ahead of him, held by the arms of Afghans who were covered in the blood and muck of a war that never ended, was his father.

Asif was carried to a row of dead bodies and gently settled in place beside a young girl in jeans and a Mickey Mouse sweatshirt.

Rafi stood, then knelt by his father's body.

He looked at his father's face, a face that had infinite love for himself and his mother. He looked at the man who had helped his mother stay alive when they were children, alone and lost in the Afghan wilderness. He saw the man who sang a thousand songs, knew a thousand stories and told a thousand bad jokes. Rafi held his father's hands, the hands that could fix anything, no matter how broken or clogged with sand. He thought about the man who had been by his side every day of his life, who was now gone and would never be with him again.

He would never come to New York City. He would never see Rafi dance on a big New York stage.

Rafi sat by his father's body and cried.

He cried for his father, who loved to be alive.

He cried for his mother, who would be devastated. He cried for himself.

And he cried for Afghanistan, which kept getting kicked in the stomach, every time it tried to get back on its feet.

13

❝ Rafi! I am looking for a boy named Rafi!"

The voice calling his name reached Rafi's ears, but it meant nothing. Nothing meant anything anymore.

"Rafi! Asif! Maryam!" the voice continued. "I am looking for three people traveling together — Rafi, Asif and Maryam. I am a friend of Mrs. Weera."

"Over here! Over here!"

Maryam was on her feet, waving her arms. Rafi didn't care.

"You are Maryam?" a young man asked.

"Yes. And this is Rafi."

The man crouched down by Rafi. "Your mother heard the news of the explosion and called us to come looking for you. What is your mother's name, son? I need to make sure you are the people I am looking for."

Rafi didn't answer. Couldn't answer.

"Look at me." The man spoke sharply, sounding so much like his mother when she was having no nonsense that Rafi raised his eyes. The man had kind eyes and the beginnings of a beard.

"What is your mother's name?" he asked again.

"Parvana," he whispered.

"Then this is the right family." He stood. "How are you holding up?" he asked Maryam.

"I need to get out of here," Maryam said. "I'm not supposed to be here. I'm supposed to be in New York."

"Do not lose hope," the young man said. "The airlift has been interrupted, not ended. Where is Asif?"

Maryam burst into tears.

"Rafi," the man said. "On your feet."

Rafi obeyed him.

"Do you know where your father is?"

Rafi nodded, and lowered his eyes. He pointed in the direction of a row of bodies under tarps.

"Show me," the friend of Mrs. Weera directed. He took Rafi's hand and Rafi took Maryam's, and they made their way over to where the bombing casualties were laid out.

The lower part of the legs of the dead were sticking out from the tarps. Rafi knew his father by his one shoe, even though it was covered with muck that had dried in the sun.

"Stay right here," the young man said. "I will be back in a moment. Don't move."

Rafi did not watch the man go. He stood at his father's one foot and one leg and held his aunt's hand.

The man was not gone long. He returned with two more men.

"These men will take care of your father's body," he said, "according to the wishes of your mother. Rafi, have you talked to your mother?"

Rafi shook his head. How could he tell his mother that his father was dead?

"Maryam, do you want to tell your sister?"

"Our phone is dead," Maryam said. "And no, I can't be the one to tell her. I just can't."

"Very well," said the young man. "I will call her."

He stepped away as the two men stood with Asif and Maryam and said a prayer over Asif's body.

When the young man returned, he nodded to his companions to take Asif away. Rafi watched them gently pick up his father. Then Aunt Maryam turned his face to her so he wouldn't have to see anymore.

"Your mother said you are to get on a plane," said the friend of Mrs. Weera. "Come with me. Nothing will be happening at this gate for the next while."

Rafi had no strength left to do anything but obey as the man led them away from the dead, away from the gully full of sewage and away from the airport fence. He paid no attention to where he was being taken. He just put one foot in front of the other.

They arrived at a bare cement yard next to a cell-phone shop. Tarps strung overhead provided shade for the people sitting on benches and lying on the ground. Some were bleeding. Some were roughly bandaged.

"Sit here," the man said.

Rafi and Maryam sat on a bench. A woman came with some water for them to drink and water in a basin for them to wash their hands and faces. A man in a Red Crescent uniform asked if they needed medical care. They said no, but he flashed a light in their eyes anyway and swabbed the small cuts on Rafi's face and arms.

Maryam asked about a way to recharge the battery on the cell phone.

"I can help you with that," the Red Crescent worker said. "Come with me."

Rafi watched his aunt follow the medic through the courtyard of people and into the back door of the shop.

He had no energy for curiosity as he looked at the people around him. The weeping, the wounded, the blank stares of the shell-shocked. He saw himself in all of those faces.

He saw himself in the woman holding her arms across her chest as if she was still holding the baby that was supposed to be there. He saw himself in the old man with the bloodstained shalwar kameez and the gash across his face that had turned his beard red. He was the woman rocking in the corner, her chador over her head and shoulders, making a constant low, wailing sound that was like a cry for help she knew would never be answered. He was the boy his age sitting on the floor with his knees to his chin, moving a piece of brick along the cement like it was a toy car, back and forth, back and forth.

Rafi thought about the ballet school he'd been accepted into, in a bright, shiny building in a bright, shiny city. He thought of the photos he'd seen and the videos on the internet of smiling children pointing their toes, leaping in front of a mirror, laughing over full plates of dinner, taking bows in costumes on a big stage.

He was supposed to be one of those children.

It was too late for that now.

He wasn't a child any longer.

Rafi got up from the bench and sat beside the boy with the broken brick.

"What's your name?" he asked.

"Samar."

"I'm Rafi. Where are your parents?"

The boy didn't look up. He kept moving the brick back and forth, back and forth.

"Look at me when I'm talking to you!" Rafi made his voice sound bossy like his mother's.

The boy looked at him.

"My father died in the explosion," Rafi said. "Did your parents die, too?"

Samar nodded.

"Were you supposed to get on a plane?"

Samar nodded again.

"To America? Do you have family in America?"

"I have an uncle in Seattle."

Rafi stood up. "Take my hand," he said.

The boy did. Rafi pulled him to his feet, then picked up the brick. Boy and brick sat beside Rafi on the bench.

Aunt Maryam returned. She looked at Samar but didn't ask any questions.

Someone handed them pieces of nan and glasses of tea. They ate and they drank. No one felt like talking.

14

Parvana threw steaming water on the wooden table and started to scrub.

"The girls can do that," Shauzia said. "Damsa, come and do this, will you?"

"Leave me alone," said Parvana.

Damsa was sweeping on the other side of the dining area. She didn't stop moving the broom, but her attention was on the two women.

"Put the cloth down, Parvana," Shauzia urged. "Come and sit. Damsa will bring you tea."

"Stop it!" Parvana yelled. "You're trying to turn me into my mother—and I am NOT my mother!"

"No one's trying to—"

"When Papa was arrested, Mama fell apart. She lay on the toshak and did nothing—nothing—while the baby cried and we ran out of food. She made herself helpless, and that's what you're trying to make me into, someone helpless and pathetic."

Shauzia looked over at Damsa. Damsa swept faster so Shauzia wouldn't think she was listening, but of course she was. The whole compound was.

"Damsa, leave the sweeping for now, will you?" Shauzia asked her. "Give us a minute."

"I have nothing," Parvana wailed, as if Shauzia had not spoken. "I've spent my whole life dancing on the edge of a knife, trying to keep people safe. And now my husband is dead and my child is off to America to be raised by Nooria! What was I thinking, letting him go? Nooria doesn't deserve him. I have no career. I have nothing. All those years of struggle and hope. Hope? Hope is a poison. Here." She thrust a teacup at Shauzia. "Go fill this with poison. I'll drink it. It would taste better than hope."

Shauzia took the cup and put it gently down in the kitchen, just as Parvana threw the empty cleaning bucket at the wall. It bounced off the wall and rolled around on the floor.

"What was the point of all that struggle?" Parvana asked. "He walked with me across Afghanistan on one leg, and he dies in a sewer? What kind of world allows people to do that? Nothing we have done has made one bit of difference, and now I have nothing!"

Shauzia slammed the flat of her hand down on the wet table. From the sound it made, Damsa thought Shauzia must have felt the impact of that slam all the way up her arm and into the center of her teeth.

"You have work," Shauzia said. "You have a legacy of people whose lives you have saved, people who are living and working and building because you saved them! You have what everybody else in this country has who is still above the ground. You have work and pain and hunger and sometimes beauty. You also have a house full of people who love you and who will see you through this."

Shauzia fetched the bucket from the floor and placed it gently in front of Parvana.

"Scrub if you want," Shauzia said gently. "Do whatever you need to. We're here. And, Parvana — this is not the hardest thing you have ever had to do."

At that, Parvana started to cry — great gulping cries. Shauzia held her as she sobbed. Damsa set her broom quietly against the wall and left the room.

She went in search of the other girls. She didn't feel like being alone.

She found them all in the small lounge, sitting together on the toshaks. They shifted over to make room for her to sit with them. Damsa sat among the three sisters. She put her arms around them and held them as they cried.

They stayed that way until Old Mrs. Musharef stood up and said even if they were sad, food had to be cooked, gardens had to be weeded and all sorts of other chores had to be done, and Asif would be the first to say that, so on your feet.

Damsa was chopping tomatoes when the pounding began at the gate.

"Open up!" a male voice shouted. "This is the authorities. Open this gate!"

Old Mrs. Musharef turned off the burners on the stove. Parvana and Shauzia ran into the kitchen.

"Hide the books," said Parvana. "Shauzia and Damsa, into the wall."

"You can't face them alone," Shauzia protested.

"I'm not alone. Damsa's from this area and her father could have sent someone to get her. And there are a whole bunch of people who would like to see you dead, Officer Shauzia. We're all safer if you're in the wall. Older girls, burqas. Younger girls, head scarves. Remember our drills."

The pounding continued at the gate. "Open this door!"

Officer Shauzia grabbed Damsa's hand and pulled her into the big lounge. As they strode across the room, Larmina at their side, Damsa saw carpets being flipped back and hidden doors built into the floor lifted up. Girls shoved books into the horizontal bookshelves built into the floor and flipped the rugs back in place.

Shauzia bent down to help them, and Damsa did the same.

"Stay calm," Shauzia told the girls. "Breathe. Act bored. It's all going to be fine."

The pounding grew louder and more insistent.

"I'm coming," yelled Old Mrs. Musharef in a weird old-lady voice as she headed out the door and into the yard. "You don't need to break down the door. Show a little respect."

Larmina opened the door on the large cupboard and took out stacks of blankets and removed two of the shelves. She slid open a door in the back.

"Follow me," said Shauzia. She crawled through the secret opening. Damsa watched her drop down out of sight.

"Go!" said Larmina. "I have to put the shelves back."

Damsa did what Shauzia had done. The last thing she saw before the cupboard door closed was a glimpse through the window of Old Mrs. Musharef hobbling with a walking stick, which she generally did not use, masquerading as a bent-over old lady, coughing and making her way slowly to the door in the gate.

Shauzia slid the secret door shut, then opened it again a little bit so they could hear what was happening. She turned on a flashlight hanging from the wall.

Damsa's mouth fell open.

There was a whole room behind the wall. It was narrow but ran the length of the lounge. There were toshaks and pillows, neatly folded blankets and two vents bringing in air from the outside.

"Parvana designed everything," Shauzia whispered back. "There are hidden spaces all over the compound. Hidden doors in the walls, too. You never know when you're going to need to escape."

She held her finger to her lips then, so there would be no more talking.

Damsa heard the sounds of people coming into the room.

"Salaam alaikum," she heard Parvana say, in a voice so mild and calm, it was shocking.

"These men think they can barge into somebody's home whenever they feel like it," said Old Mrs. Musharef in a cackly voice Damsa had never heard her use before. "The manners of young people today! You boys should be ashamed of yourselves! Wipe your feet!"

"You are with the Taliban," said Parvana. "You are welcome. Would you like some tea?"

"We would like to see your husband."

"So would I," said Parvana, sounding mildly annoyed. "But you know how men are when they are off on a trip. They lose all track of time."

"Where is he?" demanded the man's voice. "What kind of man is he to leave all these women and girls alone to get into trouble?"

"He is doing some shopping, gathering supplies. He went to the countryside somewhere to order firewood for the winter. I told him the winter is far off, but he insisted. Who am I to argue?"

"Don't listen to her," cackled Old Mrs. Musharef. "All she does is argue. My son does everything to provide for her and nothing is good enough. She didn't even want me to live with them, can you believe that? Wanted to throw me out with the trash. So, are you the new government? I told you to wipe your feet! All the sweeping I have to do!"

"We are not interested in your domestic problems," Damsa heard a man say. "We are looking for two fugitives. One is a police officer. The other is an escaped bride who has brought shame upon her family. Her name is Damsa and she is fifteen years old. People in the neighborhood say this is a place that hides girls from their families."

"We take in widows and orphans only," said Parvana. "It is our duty."

"Who pays you to do this?"

"My husband is a very good mechanic," Parvana said. "He can repair any engine. He works at the shop at the end of the lane. The owner can speak for him."

"We could use a good mechanic," Damsa heard another man say. "The Americans left us a lot of broken vehicles."

"My husband would be happy to serve," Parvana said.

"He'd be happier if you paid him," said Old Mrs. Musharef gruffly. "Volunteering is fine, but why can't a man buy his mother nice things? I don't remember the last time he bought me something new. Wastes all his money on her and these orphans! Maybe you could talk some sense into him, you being the government and all."

"Let me see your papers."

Parvana opened the cupboard Damsa and Shauzia were hiding behind. Damsa heard her remove something from a shelf.

The Taliban soldiers went through the names in the box. Damsa didn't recognize any of them.

"Where is your husband's identification?"

"He took it with him, of course," said Parvana.

She put the box of ID cards back on the shelf, then closed the cupboard door with a click.

"When will your husband be back?"

"Two days or three," Parvana said. "I hear many roadblocks are slowing things down. Perhaps you could do something about that?"

"Don't concern yourself with roadblocks," the Talib said. "Concern yourself with staying out of trouble."

"I tell her that all the time," whined Old Mrs. Musharef. "If she spent her time learning to cook a decent meal we'd all be better off."

"Our soldiers have been fighting for a long time," said a Talib. "In victory, they deserve wives. Have any of these girls been promised?"

"They all have," Parvana said. "My husband meets many people through his work of fixing cars. He prides himself on the marriage arrangements he makes."

"Perhaps the promises are not as solid as you think," said the Talib.

"That is my husband's affair," Parvana said lightly, as if the matter was of no consequence to her.

"He will be back in three days?" asked a Talib. "Then we will be back in three days. If your husband is not back by then, we will assume he has abandoned his family and we will act accordingly. Salaam alaikum."

Damsa heard them leave the house, trailed by Old Mrs. Musharef who went on and on about her bad back and if they were now the government, couldn't they do something about all the pain she was in?

Damsa peered through the air vents and saw the Taliban soldiers looking around the yard, pointing at things and nodding their heads, Old Mrs. Musharef sticking to them like a mosquito.

Finally, they left.

Old Mrs. Musharef bolted the door behind them. She waited until they drove away before unbending herself to her full height, stretching her back with the walking stick across her shoulders, and heading back into the house.

Shauzia pulled the sliding door open as the wardrobe door opened, too. Shelves were taken out, and Shauzia and Damsa tumbled into the big room. They joined the others in applauding their success in deceiving the Taliban.

"I hate hiding," Shauzia said.

"It's better than the alternative," said Larmina.

"Three days," said Parvana. "Three days."

15

" It's not my fault."

Maryam got that out right away. The day was stressful enough without Parvana going all Big Sister on her.

"We're in the airport," she added quickly. "We're waiting to board. I have to make this short because we could start boarding at any minute."

She listened a moment, then said, "Of course you want to talk to Rafi. He's not within arm's reach just now. You don't know what it's been like for us. You can't even imagine. We had to crawl through sewer water! And then the explosion! Really, Parvana, you cannot imagine it, even if you tried your whole life...

"No, they're putting us on a military flight. Heaven knows what the seats will be like, and certainly no movie, but you'll hear no complaints from me. Anyway, it will be a short flight. They're taking us to Qatar first. After that, I guess we'll get put on a flight to New York. Nooria will have to figure that out. I can't be expected to do everything.

"Yes, yes, yes, you want to talk to Rafi. Parvana, I don't want you to worry. You are my sister, and as soon as I get to New York I'll make Nooria start on your visa application. It should be easier now that you're a widow.

"How is that insensitive? It's the truth, and you weren't there, I was. You should be having some compassion for me.

"Yes, right, Rafi. I'm getting to that. Look, is Shauzia there? Let me talk to Shauzia. She's easier to talk to than you are.

"All right! All right! But let me say again, I didn't do anything wrong. He's your son, and he's just as bullheaded as you are. I'm only his aunt. You can't blame me.

"I'm trying to tell you! Quit interrupting me. Are you sure I can't talk to Shauzia?

"All right. Well, first let me say, Rafi is fine. At least, I assume he is.

"Here's what happened.

"He picked up this strange boy when we were at that rest place where the Friends of Mrs. Weera took us. Quiet boy. Polite. Named Samar. His parents were killed in the bombing at the airport fence. He was supposed to go live with his uncle in Seattle.

"I'm trying to tell you!

"So, Rafi had this boy, this Samar, tagging right along with us outside the airport gate this morning.

Same crush of people, although Mrs. Weera's Friends made sure we were at the right gate and not too far back.

"The American soldiers were checking papers before letting anyone inside. We were maybe six families back. Rafi takes that document pouch off his neck and hands it to me.

"Then he takes the hand of that stray boy, Samar, and puts that boy's hand into my hand.

"'This is Rafi,' he says, like you can just exchange one child for another.

"'What are you doing?' I asked him. We had to whisper because we were getting closer and closer to the soldiers at the gate.

"'My father is dead,' says Rafi. 'I need to be with my mother. Dancing can wait.' Dancing can wait! After all the work I put into him. He is such a disappointment.

"Yes, of course I argued with him. But I couldn't force him. Did you want me to make a scene and have the soldiers think I was trying to force a child to go with me? Really, Parvana, you're safe in your little make-believe Green Valley world. You should see what it's like out here in the real world.

"This stray boy, this Samar, kept repeating, 'I am Rafi, Aunt Maryam. I am Rafi, Aunt Maryam.' Your son planned this thing long before we got to the airport gate and then he sprang it on me when he knew it would be too late for me to properly argue with him.

"Well, he started to leave, and we were almost at the gate now, just two families ahead of us. Try to imagine the scene, Parvana, and have some sympathy for me. Rafi—the real Rafi—started to leave. I grabbed his arm and then—you'll be proud of me for this, Parvana—I took off all my gold chains and put them around his neck and hid them under his shirt.

"What do you mean, what then? I just gave him all the money I've earned as a singer, and you don't say thank you? It's a loan then, Parvana, and I expect you to pay me back.

"I'm trying to tell you.

"Rafi just melted away into the crowd. He just disappeared. I went through the gate with the child who was formerly named Samar and is now the new Rafi, and we are about to get on a gigantic military cargo plane with hundreds of other people and go to Qatar. I don't know when we will get to New York.

"Of course I'm keeping the new Rafi with me! He's my nephew now, aren't you, New Rafi? I must say, he has much less attitude than the old Rafi. Yes, we'll sort it all out when we get to New York, and when I say we, I mean Nooria.

"Look, Parvana, I've got to go. They're telling us to line up.

"Oh, one last thing. Just before he ran off, Rafi said to me, 'Tell Mama I'm coming home.'"

Maryam ended the call.

"That went better than I thought it would," she said to the new Rafi. "Parvana thinks I can't do anything difficult, but I did that phone call, didn't I? I have handled the passports and the papers all this time, haven't I? Parvana thinks she knows everything, but she doesn't."

Maryam took hold of Samar/Rafi's hand, and they joined the line of people waiting to get on the plane.

"Do you like music, new Rafi?" she asked. "Ever hear 'Almond Trees in Bloom'? It's one of my biggest hits."

16

Rafi was on a roof.

He'd run away from the airport, not daring to look back even one time in case that made him change his mind. And he could not change it, no matter how much he wanted to.

Rafi ran without direction, up one street and down another, hopping on and off curbs, dodging cars and pickup trucks full of rifle-carrying Taliban soldiers. He ran past fruit sellers and a man selling Taliban flags, white with scriptures written on them in black. He ran past families making their slow way to the airport, loaded down with luggage and children, their faces scrunched with worry and fear. He ran looking for his father's car, panicking that he couldn't remember where they'd left it, and only stopping the search when he remembered he couldn't drive, even if he'd had the car keys.

He didn't know what made him run into the banquet hall. Maybe it was just that the door was propped open like an invitation. He didn't stop to think about it. He just went inside.

When he saw the stairs, he started to climb them. Three stories, his legs already sore from running and his body already exhausted from the ordeal of the past few days.

Up, up, up he climbed, until he opened the last door and stepped out onto the flat roof.

He could see the airport from there.

Rafi felt his Aunt Maryam's gold chains against the skin of his chest and felt so proud that he was her nephew. His mother would stretch that gold into cash and stretch that cash into food and shelter and rescue for many, many others. He would help her. He would keep a strict list of what they spent the money on, so he could write to his aunt and tell her everything her gift had done.

And he would pay her back. He'd find a way. When he became a professional dancer…

That's when it hit him, what he had given up.

He doubled over with sadness.

He would never dance around New York City, leaping from rooftop to rooftop.

He would never go to that bright, shiny school where real dance teachers would correct his positions and teach him new steps and tell him to straighten his shoulders.

He would never wear costumes full of color and light and he would not dance on a big New York stage.

The new Rafi, Samar, would have the wonderful new life in America.

Twisted with jealousy and regret, Rafi wrapped his arms around his chest.

What had he done? He had thrown his future away.

He heard the roar of a plane and got to his feet.

He watched the massive military cargo plane lift from the runway and somehow become airborne. All that steel and iron, with its belly full of frightened people, taking to the air like a giant bird.

Rafi spread his arms like wings and rose up on his toes right up into the air beside that plane. He flew beside it, seeing his aunt and Samar inside, and when it circled high over Kabul, Rafi circled with it. He looked down at the city of troubles, at its mountains and its sorrows, and left it all behind as he disappeared into a cloud.

Then the plane was out of sight and Rafi was still on the roof.

Just a boy, all alone in a city he didn't know, very far from home.

17

Damsa was in charge of backpacks.

"Lay everything out in groups," Larmina suggested. "Then go down the line. That's the easiest way to make sure everyone's got some of everything."

"Everything" meant the supplies they would need for the journey ahead — food, water, flashlights, shawls, and so on. Damsa's job was to collect all they had in each category, divide it by the number of people and put those things into each backpack.

"Once they're packed, hand them out," said Larmina. "We'll each put in any small personal things we want to take."

Larmina's voice caught. Damsa watched her face work very hard to keep from crying.

"All right?" Larmina asked, meaning, Are you all right if I leave you with this important task? Will it be done properly?

"All right," Damsa replied and got started.

Larmina left Damsa with a list that she'd worked out with Shauzia, along with where to find everything. Larmina also left her with a pen to check off each item as it was gathered and again when it was in the packs.

Damsa gathered little first-aid kits from the cupboard with the secret door. These were small hand-sewn bags containing bandages, a few aspirin and alcohol swabs. She put these little bags at one end of the long dining table and put her first check mark on the list.

She counted out flashlights and batteries, packets of nuts and packets of crackers, dried fruit in twisted paper pouches and bags of hard candies. Each backpack got an extra shawl that could be used as a blanket, three small boxes of juice with straws attached, four bottles of water, and a small notebook with a pen.

Items were checked off, then checked again when they went into the backpacks.

All done. Twelve backpacks for twelve people. One of those people was a baby. Damsa guessed they'd all take turns carrying that pack.

She looked around for someone to say, "Good job," and tell her what to do next. But of course everyone was busy doing other things.

Damsa had enjoyed packing the backpacks. She went looking for another task.

She found Hadiah in the big lounge, taking books out of the horizontal bookshelves built into the floor.

"What are you doing?" Damsa asked her.

"Parvana told me to choose, but I can't," said Hadiah. "We need all of them. *I* need all of them."

"They're just books," said Damsa. "You can always get more."

"Can I? I never could before. I'm not leaving them any of them behind." Hadiah shuffled around so that her back was to Damsa. Damsa tried to talk to her again, but Hadiah ignored her.

Damsa let her be. She walked over to Parvana's office. Parvana and Shauzia were both on cell phones and computers, talking in quick, staccato bursts into the phones, then to each other, then into the phones again, all the while typing on their laptops. Damsa waited for them to acknowledge her, but it was like she was invisible.

Damsa went into her dormitory. Larmina was on her bunk, clothes and objects laid out the bed in front of her. There was a stuffed bear, a small wooden keepsake box beautifully carved and painted, a bird made from bits of metal, three well-used notebooks and a globe.

"I don't know what to take," Larmina said. "I can't take all of it, but I don't want to leave anything behind for *them*. The Taliban doesn't deserve any of my things."

Damsa sat on her own bunk. She had no things, not anymore. If she had the opportunity to go back to her old house and choose what to take with her, how would she decide? The things that were the most beautiful? The ones that cost the most? The things that had no value to anyone but her, like the piece of quartz she picked out of the dirt on her way home from school and was too pretty to throw away.

"Tell me about your things," Damsa suggested to Larmina.

Larmina started with the bear.

"Parvana gave this to me the first night I was here. Asif made me this box for my birthday last year." She ran her fingertips over the carved flowers, stained slightly redder than the rest of the box. She held up the little bird. "I made this. It's the first thing I ever welded."

The notebooks were full of her poetry.

"It's not good poetry," Larmina said, "but it's mine. It's what I was thinking and feeling at the time. Am I just supposed to throw those thoughts and feelings away? Leave them for the Taliban, who will trample them to dust? And this," she picked up the globe. "I bought this with money I earned sewing bookmarks for the gift shops in Kabul. I saw it at the stationery store. As soon as I saw it, I wanted it. I saved for so long! When I finally bought it, I carried it around for a week. I felt like I was holding the whole world."

"Why not take it all?" Damsa asked.

"We might be walking," said Larmina. "Parvana and Shauzia are trying to find someone who will take us in his truck, but that's a lot to ask. We'd have to tell lies at all the checkpoints. We have false ID for everyone, but Parvana says the Taliban are better educated this time than they were the first time they took over. They can read. They can use technology.

Any man driving us would be in danger, which means we would be in danger. Even if we get a ride part of the way, we won't get one the whole way. Parvana says we can take only what we can carry easily. All us girls and women traveling together. It's going to draw attention. We have to be able to run."

"Hadiah wants to take all the books."

"Damsa, I know you are trying to help me right now, but if I have to say goodbye to my things, I'd like to do it in private."

Damsa left Larmina with her things. What else could she do?

Just outside the room, Damsa turned back and asked Larmina, "Where are we going?"

"Parvana and Shauzia are trying to figure that out." She picked up the globe and wrapped her arms around it. Damsa turned away.

The day dragged on in a mixture of frantic activity, worry and sorrow. Damsa helped out where she could. She was beginning to understand that she could see a job that needed to be done and she could go ahead and do it, without asking permission first. She sat with Zahra and helped her choose what things she'd need for her baby.

"I have lots of room in my backpack," Damsa said. "I can carry anything you don't have space for."

They decided Damsa should carry extra diapers, soap and the cereal biscuits the baby liked to chew on. Damsa filled her pack, then set it aside.

Old Mrs. Musharef was helping the two new little girls, so Damsa helped her, finding small socks in Green Valley's supply of clothing. She rolled up and tied the comfort blankets they'd grown used to. She attached them to the backpacks through the arm straps and made them secure. The small blankets wouldn't add much weight, and the little girls would be happier having them close.

All around Green Valley, the girls and women moved and worked with serious purpose. Damsa helped Zahra pick chamomile flowers in case anyone had tummy troubles on the journey and needed soothing tea. She worked with Larmina to package up what they could from the pantry. Anything they didn't take, they would give to their neighbors. The same with the vegetables now ready in the garden. Damsa twisted tomatoes off the stems and brushed soil from onions and leeks.

Late in the afternoon, she joined Parvana and Old Mrs. Musharef. They went out the gate and down the path to the little village, each carrying bags of things to give away—things that were too valuable to leave for the Taliban but too much to take on their trip. They left a bag full of vegetables, handicrafts and Asif-made toys with the poorest families. These families could eat the vegetables and sell the other things to buy more food or pay their rent.

They didn't tell anyone they were leaving. The villagers were used to getting things from Parvana. They didn't ask questions. They just said thank you.

Damsa was very tired when they got back and the gate was bolted behind them, but she helped prepare supper, then sat with everyone at the table.

Almost everyone.

"Should we wait for Parvana?" Larmina asked.

"Let's go ahead and eat," said Old Mrs. Musharef. "Parvana knows where to find us."

They ate quietly. It had been a long day of sorting and packing. There had even been a bonfire in the yard, where Parvana and Shauzia burned the files and record books that contained information that could identify the girls and women they had helped, as well as the many women and men who had helped with those rescues.

Damsa was sure all ears were listening for the Taliban pounding at the gate. They weren't due until the next day, but no one trusted that. Everyone knew this was their last supper in Green Valley. They also knew that whatever the next day brought, it would not be easy.

In this sad silence, Old Mrs. Musharef started to sing an old Afghan folk song. Its notes and rhythms were as familiar as breathing and as comforting as the moon. Everyone joined in.

When the song was over, there was Parvana.

She held a bundle of Asif and Rafi's clothes.

She asked Damsa, Larmina and Hadiah to come and stand by her.

"We need to do all we can to keep everyone safe," Parvana said. She looked from one girl to another. "I have a question for each of you. How attached are you to your hair?"

18

R afi opened his eyes.
       It was morning. He had made it through the night. He was alive.

He slowly unwound himself from the tablecloth he'd borrowed from the banquet hall laundry cart. It made a good blanket. He raised himself up on his elbows and looked around at where he was.

After leaving the roof, Rafi had just walked. He knew he was walking away from the airport, but he had no idea if the streets were taking him deeper into Kabul or somehow closer to home.

He'd walked until it got dark. Then he took shelter in the first place that looked at least halfway safe. He took the folded-up tablecloth out of his grandfather's shoulder bag, wrapped himself up in it, using the shoulder bag as a pillow, and instantly fell asleep.

Now, in the morning light, he could see he was in a small wooden hut with shelves stocked with packets of chips and boxes of fruit drinks.

The door was wide open, but why hadn't it been closed and locked, with all of these snacks just sitting on the shelves? The owner must have forgotten to lock it, or maybe he had been in too much of a hurry. Maybe the Taliban were coming after him, although why the Taliban would be interested in a chip seller, Rafi didn't know.

The shelf full of chips looked tempting. More tempting than the fruit drinks, even though Rafi was thirsty as well as hungry. But while his mother might sometimes let him have fruit drinks, she almost never let him have chips.

"If you don't acquire a taste for junk food, you will never miss it," she said.

Too late, Rafi thought. He already liked chips, and whenever he had the chance to go to a shop by himself—which was rare—and if he had any money in his pocket, he always bought himself a bag of chips. He ate them before he got home, so that he wouldn't have to share them or answer for them.

And now here he was, far from his mother, looking at a shelf full of potato chips, with no one around to stop him from taking them! All he had to do was open his grandfather's shoulder bag and stuff it full.

But he couldn't do it. Sure, he'd stolen a tablecloth (borrowed it, but he doubted the banquet hall would see it that way), but only because he needed something to use as a blanket. And his mother would help him return the tablecloth, washed and pressed. She'd insist on it.

He didn't need the chips to survive. He still had some nuts and fruit in his bag.

Rafi wanted his mother to be proud of him. When he got back to Green Valley, he wanted to be able to tell her all about his trip. He knew he'd be ashamed to tell her he'd stolen some chips, so he left them on the shelf.

Into the quiet of the snack hut came the sound of trucks and men's voices. The voices were not angry. In fact, they sounded happy. Rafi heard laughter.

The hut had two small doors above the counter that could be pulled open to make a serving area. Rafi pulled them open just slightly and peered through to see what was going on.

He saw two pickup trucks, each one filled to the brim with Taliban soldiers.

Rafi wanted to run, but he was scared that they would see him.

He watched as the soldiers got out of their trucks and started to walk around. That's when he really took in where he was, and where he had spent the night.

He was in an amusement park.

What's more, he had been in this park before! On his one trip to Kabul with his parents, this was one of the places they had gone. It had been the best day! Of course, his mother had talked to all the women and to all the children begging, asking their names and what their lives were like. And, of course, his father had talked to the ride operators to find out how the rides worked when all Rafi wanted to do was get on the rides and have fun.

But, looking back, that had all been part of the greatness of the day.

Rafi looked out at the colorful rides and felt a deep aching for his parents.

He watched the Taliban wander among the rides, running their hands over them, pointing to the giant teapot and laughing. They got into the big teacups that surrounded the huge teapot and sat down. They looked like they were waiting for something to happen.

Some of the men were looking at the engine, trying this or that, trying to make it all work, but not having any success.

Rafi watched it all, fascinated.

"What have we here?"

Rafi spun around. A tall Talib stood in the open door of the hut, his gray beard and lined face making him look much older than the young men at the teacup ride. He towered over Rafi.

"What are you doing here, boy?" the Talib asked. "Stealing?"

Rafi shook all over. That Talib could probably kill him with one swoop of his hand.

"Speak up! You have a voice, don't you? You're an Afghan, aren't you? Speak up and be proud. This is a time to be proud. Unless you are stealing. Are you stealing?"

Rafi managed to shake his head, no.

"Let me see that bag," said the Talib.

Rafi put it behind him.

"Hand it over," the Talib ordered. "If you are stealing, it will not go well for you. We want an Afghanistan where no one steals from anyone else, don't we? So, prove that you are honest."

Rafi's arms moved the bag slightly in the Talib's direction.

"It belonged to my grandfather," Rafi said in a very small voice.

The Talib took the bag and emptied it out. "Snacks and juice but different from the snacks and juice sold here. One bottle of water. And one book. Why do you have this book?

The Talib shook it in Rafi's face.

"It is an English book. What is the name of it? Why are you reading such books?"

The book was *To Kill a Mockingbird*, but Rafi did not tell him that. Instead, he said, "It belonged to my mother."

"And where is your mother?"

Rafi made a gesture that could have meant the next town or the next world.

The Talib handed him back the shoulder bag but kept hold of the book. He knelt down beside Rafi.

"My mother is dead, too," the Talib said. "We all miss our mothers, don't we?"

He handed Rafi the book.

"Burn this," he said. "Don't let us find it on you again. I'm being gentle with you today in memory of my mother. Do not think for a moment that means I am not serious."

He rose up to his full height and stared down at Rafi.

"If you are not stealing, what are you doing here?" the Talib asked.

A word came into Rafi's head then—a word so perfect for the situation, it was like his mother and father opened his brain and stuck it in there.

"Protecting," he said.

"Good for you," said the Talib. "Is your father in charge of this park? Is he around? My men would like to go for a ride. They are good at fighting. Not so good with mechanical things."

"My father is not here just now," said Rafi. He put the book back in the shoulder bag and put the bag's strap across his chest. He was feeling slightly stronger now, and steadier.

"Do you know how to get these rides started? My men deserve a celebration. I'd rather they not fire off their guns into the air. Too many gunshots, people stop paying attention. When a gun is fired in this part of Kabul, *my* part, I want it to scare people into doing what's right. That way we can all have a better life, yes?"

"My father told me all about the rides," Rafi said. "I can try to start them up for you."

The Talib commander led him out into the park and got into one of the teacups with his men.

Faced with the controls, Rafi reached back into his memory. He opened the control panel and turned on the power. Then he pressed the button that made the ride go. He watched as the big teacups full of cheering young Talibs picked up speed and spun around and around and around.

And then he left. Quickly.

Eventually, someone would figure out how to make the ride stop.

Until then, a Talib twirling in a giant teacup was a Talib not out in the world doing something bad.

But they would be mad after spinning around for a long time, and the commander knew his face.

Rafi needed to get out of Kabul.

Now.

19

Parvana closed the gate on the now-empty compound and bolted it shut. She was all alone.

It had not been easy persuading Shauzia to leave with the others. It had not been easy for any of them to leave her behind. She knew that. But they had to get away, and she could not leave until her son came home. That's just the way it was.

The silence was nice.

Parvana had not had much quiet time in her life. There was always so much to do, so many people to take care of, so much to worry about. Even in the jail cell, when she was a teenager and captured by the American military, she did not have much quiet. The Americans bombarded her with a song about a dog, over and over and over, at a loud volume. It was a way the Americans had of trying to make her talk.

It didn't work. Parvana was stronger than that.

She learned much later that the song was called "Puppy Love," sung by a boy named Donny Osmond. Now and then she heard it on the radio. It only took a couple of notes to make Parvana feel like she was right back in that cell.

The last few hours in Green Valley had been chaotic, even with all their organizing skills and all the helping hands. Parvana was so proud of the girls! Even though they were scared, and even though they had been through so much in their young lives, they all pitched in and worked together.

Parvana sat on the bench in Leila's Playground and looked out at the compound. She'd designed the bench. She and Asif had built it together. It had two seats — one facing the playground, one facing the compound. Each view took in gardens full of color.

"Let's cut all the gardens down!" Larmina had declared before the girls left. Larmina, who had never been allowed out of her home by her father, a man who had arranged a marriage for her while she was still a baby, who kept her from studying and singing and sunshine. Larmina had taken to Green Valley like she was made for it, learning how things grew, how words worked, how freedom worked. "Let's not leave any beauty for the Taliban."

That was what Larmina wanted, and the other girls nodded.

"What if they bring their wives here?" Parvana asked the girls. "What if they bring their children, their young sons and daughters? It has to be a difficult life, being family members of someone in the Taliban. Perhaps the beauty of this place will even soften the hearts of the Taliban who take it over. When you know beauty, it is harder to destroy things."

Parvana was not sure if she believed that anymore, but the girls accepted it. She was glad they did. There was no way she was going to allow a pebble of what they had created here to be destroyed. The girls needed to remember it as they had lived it. Parvana needed that, too.

She did not know how much time she had before the Taliban arrived. They'd said three days, but nothing in Parvana's experience made her trust anything they said.

It didn't matter. The girls were out. She had done all she could to get them safely away.

It had been difficult. Anyone they knew who had a truck and could be trusted to take vulnerable, fugitive girls to a place that might be safe was already planning their own escape. Rumors were all over the place. The Taliban were not in the villages, or they were in the villages so the cities were safer, or the Taliban wouldn't dare go into that valley or that province.

Parvana knew there was no place safe for the Green Valley girls. The best they could hope for was to go to a province where none of the girls had family, and where their new identities had the best chance of holding up.

Finally, after many phone calls, one of the Friends of Mrs. Weera put her in touch with someone from the Women's Small Business Cooperative. One of their fruit growers could take them in their truck, as long as they didn't mind sitting among sacks of nectarines.

Parvana couldn't control what happened on the road, but Shauzia was the best person to see them through that, anyway. Parvana would join them with Rafi, once he showed up.

Parvana began her last walk around the compound, looking at all they had created. She carried her things bundled together in a tied-up shawl.

In the main building, she took down the photograph of Mrs. Weera and Mrs. Weera's athletic medal. She pushed them deep into her bundle.

She made herself go into Asif's workshop and run her fingertips over the rough wood. She picked up the unfinished bear from the work bench. It was the last thing he'd worked on. She loosened her bundle and tucked the bear away.

She went into the little house she'd shared with him and Rafi. She went into the main building. She knew which parts of the floor held secret bookcases. She hoped the books would remain safe, so that when the Taliban were finally out of power again, curious children would find them.

Her last stop was the lavender field of fake France, with its Eiffel Tower made from sticks. How surprised Shauzia had been when the girls brought her, blindfolded, to see it for the first time!

How she had wept—and Shauzia was not a weeper.

"Maybe one day we will see the real one, my friend," Parvana said now.

She heard the sound of trucks approaching the gate. The gate was bolted on the inside. She had time to dash to the courtyard to see the tops of the white flags, then dash back to the lavender field.

She held her bundle tightly in her fist. Then she slipped through a door hidden in the wall behind fake France. She flipped her burqa over her head and closed the door tightly behind her.

Carefully walking away from the compound walls, Parvana made a wide berth around the cultivated plots and into a thicket of trees. From there she could see the lane leading to the main road. She could also see Taliban soldiers banging at the gate of what used to be Green Valley.

Parvana sat with her back against the largest tree, hidden by weeds and shrubs, and soon looked like just one more of Afghanistan's widows, living on the street because she had nowhere else to go.

20

R afi walked down deserted streets.
Now and then a man selling fruit or sandals or
vegetables rolled his cart down the pavement, looking for customers. Sometimes Rafi saw someone buy
something, but mostly everyone stayed indoors.

"People are scared. They don't know what's going
to happen," said an onion seller when Rafi stopped
to ask for directions. "Me? I say whatever happens,
people need to eat and they need onions."

"Aren't you worried?" Rafi asked.

"I don't worry about politics. I worry about selling
my onions before they go bad. Does worrying about
politics help anybody? I sell my onions, I mind my
own business, and that way I can keep selling my
onions and minding my own business."

One of those onions took that moment to roll off
the cart and onto the street. Rafi chased after it and
brought it back to the cart.

"I'm trying to get home," he said, "but I don't
even know how to get out of Kabul. Which street do
I take?"

"Why are you so far from home?" The pedlar put the onion with the others. "Are you running away from home like the onion that ran away from my cart?"

"I'm not running away," Rafi said.

"So you say," said the pedlar. "But if you are not telling me the truth, and I help you by giving you directions, then I could be in trouble with your father by helping you run away."

"You won't have trouble from my father."

"So you say," said the pedlar again.

"You're not going to help me?"

"I'm going to sell my onions," said the pedlar.

Rafi was silent for a moment. Then he raised his arm and swiped it over the onions. They cascaded all over the pavement.

The onion seller shouted curse after curse as Rafi hurried away down the street.

Rafi was mad at the pedlar but he was madder at himself, and he was ashamed of what he had done.

He'd leave out that part of the story he told his mother about this journey, when he finally saw her again.

Rafi walked until he was so tired, hot, hungry and thirsty that he needed a break. He sat under an awning overhanging the closed door of a shoe shop and reached into his grandfather's shoulder bag. He took out a bottle of water and a little bag of dried fruit and nuts. He allowed himself one good swallow, and then just a few sips more. He chewed on some walnuts and a dried apricot.

Rafi heard a sound that was sort of a meow and sort of a tiny cry, and he went all-over cold.

His mother had told him how, when she was not much older than him, she had found a baby crying, surrounded by its dead family, all alone in a village that had been bombed. She had taken the baby with her as she walked across Afghanistan.

Rafi knew how hard it had been for her to keep that baby fed, watered, clean and safe, and she'd had Asif to do half the work.

Rafi did not want to have to take care of a baby.

I won't look, he decided. *I'll walk away and pretend I didn't hear.*

But, of course, he couldn't do that. He couldn't have two things he was ashamed to tell his mother.

Rafi's eyes followed the delicate sound. It was coming from behind a board leaning against the wall.

He got up, moved the board, and there was a little orange kitten! It had squeezed itself into the shade of the leaning board but was blocked by a flowerpot and didn't know how to get out.

"Hello," said Rafi, picking up the kitten. He felt it nestle into his chest. It gave another couple of cries, as if to tell Rafi the story of being trapped behind the board.

"I don't have any food for you," said Rafi, "but I have some water. Are you thirsty?"

He sat back down, gently disentangled the kitten's claws from his shirt and put it on the ground. He poured out a capful of water and offered it to the kitten. The kitten examined it closely, then lapped it up.

"Shauzia had a dog named Jasper when she was my age and on her own," Rafi told the kitten. "Maybe you could be my Jasper."

He scratched the kitten behind its ears.

"You found my kitty."

A small boy peered around the side of the shop. He scooted over to Rafi and scooped up the kitten.

Rafi put the cap back on the water bottle.

"Is there a grown-up with you?" he asked the little boy.

The little boy looked all around him, then shook his head.

Rafi tried again.

"Are there grown-ups inside, close by? Your parents, maybe, or someone who looks after you?"

This time the child nodded.

"Can you go and get one of them for me? Tell them I'm lost."

The little boy nodded again, then ran away, holding the kitten tightly.

Rafi waited, wondering what sort of adult would come out to see him.

It was an old man, with the little boy grinning shyly from behind his legs.

"You are lost?" the old man asked.

"I'm trying to get home, but I don't even know how to get out of Kabul."

"Any road will take you out of Kabul if you walk on it long enough," the man said. "Where are your parents?"

"I'm heading home to my mother," Rafi said. "My father was killed in the explosion at the airport."

"Wait here," the man said. He and the little boy left Rafi alone. They were back a few minutes later with a piece of stale nan and a glass of cold tea. Rafi gulped the tea and chewed at the bread.

"Go now," the old man told him, pointing. "Please. We don't want the Taliban stopping here to ask why there's a small boy outside our shop. We don't want them stopping here for any reason."

"Thank you," said Rafi. "I'll go. One more thing. Are you a Friend of Mrs. Weera?"

"I have never heard of her," the old man said.

Rafi thanked him again and left the shade of the storefront. He could feel the old man watching him leave.

He turned another corner. He was not going to risk running into the onion seller again.

21

Pomegranates made poor mattresses.

Damsa could not say she was comfortable, bumping along in the back of a truck filled with sacks of fruit, but she was having a very good time.

Yes, they were in danger. Yes, they were off to the unknown. And, yes, the days ahead promised nothing easy. But for the moment, Damsa had sun and freedom, and that was enough.

"How attached are you to your hair?" Parvana had asked.

As it turned out, Damsa wasn't attached to it at all. She was shocked at how easily she said goodbye to it.

She, Larmina and Hadiah had sat in a row on a dining-room bench. The younger girls watched as Parvana cut Damsa's hair, Shauzia cut Larmina's and Old Mrs. Musharef cut Hadiah's. The little ones giggled and clapped and cheered as Damsa and the others brushed their hands through the soft shag where their long hair used to be.

Asif's clothes were big on Damsa and Larmina, but easily fixable. Rafi's fit Hadiah almost perfectly.

"You now have pockets," Parvana said, pointing them out. "I always liked the pockets."

She put a pattu around each of their shoulders. The brown shawls would give them warmth and help keep them disguised. There were also caps for their heads.

"Not bad," Parvana told them. "You won't pass close inspection, but you look enough like boys that the Taliban won't think this is a group of women and girls out in the world alone without supervision."

She rubbed the sleeve of the kameez Damsa wore and went quiet for a moment. Damsa was sure she was remembering the man who last wore this shirt.

Then Parvana smiled.

"Thank you," she said to the three of them. "This will keep everyone safer."

Now, riding in the truck with pomegranates digging into her shoulder blades, Damsa loved the feeling of the sun in her face. Asif's clothes were comfortable, and the pattu was soft and did not show the dust.

Her leg was cramping, though. She tried moving it around but there wasn't a lot of space. Twelve people and a load of fruit made the truck very full.

Old Mrs. Musharef didn't seem to be bothered. She was right beside Damsa, sound asleep and snoring like a jet engine.

Damsa caught Larmina's eye and they grinned. Larmina's face looked strong with her new haircut. Damsa liked to think her own face looked strong, too.

In the middle of the day, the truck turned off the highway and stopped in front of the fruit co-op's warehouse. Damsa gently woke Old Mrs. Musharef and helped her climb down from the truck.

"Larmina and I will ask around for another truck that can take us farther," Shauzia said. "Damsa, you stay here and see that everyone stays together. If we get a chance at a ride and have to leave right away, I don't want to have to be looking for anyone."

After such a long ride in the truck, everyone needed to use a restroom. Damsa went up to a very busy woman with a clipboard and asked her where the facilities were.

"If I let you use my restroom, what will you do for me?"

The woman was wearing a burqa flipped back so her face was exposed. There were deep lines of worry on her forehead.

"The Taliban could shut us down at any time," the woman said. "All this food needs to be tallied so the farmers can get paid, then divided up and sent to the villages for distribution. Many of our workers did not show up today. They're afraid. They are right to be. So again I ask. What will you do for me?"

"We'll work," said Damsa, making the decision for everyone, and getting a nod of approval from Old Mrs. Musharef.

Damsa found a quiet corner for the youngest ones. They were fascinated by all the new people and activity and were content to sit and watch. The others were pressed into service. The three sisters did bagging and carrying. Hadiah counted and kept track. Damsa and Old Mrs. Musharef checked requisition forms and put orders together.

Another new thing I can do, thought Damsa.

Shauzia and Larmina returned from their search for a truck and driver, shook their heads and pitched in.

"Our trucks do not go where you are headed," the coordinator said. "Given what's going on with the Taliban, I can't ask the drivers to do more than take the food where it needs to go, then get on home to their families. But I do have this."

She pointed to a big wagon with high sides. It was like a box on wheels, with a long handle to pull it.

"The little ones can ride in this," she said. "It will make your journey a little easier. If you can return the cart someday, good. If you get a chance at a ride and need to leave the cart by the side of the road, someone will find it and make good use of it."

They thanked her, she thanked them, the youngest were lifted inside along with some bags of bruised fruit, and then they were back on the road.

—

Damsa was a cart horse.

It was hot work pulling the wagon with the small children inside. The road was not smooth. The cart's wheels kept getting stuck in the potholes. Then everyone had to be lifted out of the cart, the cart lifted out of the rut, then everyone lifted back into the cart.

"I'll pull with you," Larmina said. She'd had a turn at pulling by herself already, but she took hold of half the handle and walked alongside Damsa. With the two of them pulling, the work was easier.

"We're on an adventure," Larmina said, sounding quite cheerful about it. "Oh, I know, working at the fruit co-op was not exactly exciting, but it was different from an ordinary day."

"I liked it," Damsa agreed.

"I hated to leave Green Valley," said Larmina. "But, as Parvana said, it was our home for as long as it was our home, and when we get to our new home, we'll make a new Green Valley."

"Green Valley," Damsa said, remembering. "It was so much prettier than this road of dust."

"Don't call it that," said Larmina. "Let's give it a grand name so we'll feel grand walking along it. How about the Highway of Fine Particles?"

Damsa was about to admit that did sound grander, but just then, a cart wheel went into another pothole.

"All these craters," said Damsa. "It's like we're walking on the moon."

Damsa and Larmina looked at each other.

"Moon Walk!" they said at the same time.

They laughed and got busy, lifting the young ones out and getting the cart back on the road.

22

Rafi turned onto a street behind the street where the onion seller had been and then turned again. All the streets looked the same to him. None gave him a clue as to where he should go.

He would have to find someone else to ask.

That seemed unlikely as he now found himself in a neighborhood full of shops, all closed. He paused in the shade of one of them, but an angry voice came out at him.

"Are you trying to break into my shop?"

"What? No!"

"You are. You're a looter. I know a looter when I see one. You'd better run. If I have to come out there—"

Rafi ran. He ran farther than he needed to, just because he was tired of being where he was in this ugly, shut-up part of the city.

A truckload of Taliban soldiers stopped him. It turned into the street he was trying to cross and blocked his way.

"Why are you running, boy?" asked a Talib, a

young man with a long dark beard and a dark turban. He pointed his rifle at Rafi's chest.

"He's too small to be an enemy," said the Talib beside him. "He's too small to do anything."

"He's big enough to do our laundry," said a third. "Come on up here, boy. You can stay with us. You can do our laundry and make our tea."

Rafi didn't move. Couldn't move.

"He looks scared," said another man. "Why is he scared? He should be thanking us for saving his country. Why are you scared?"

"He was running. Did he steal something? If he stole something, we know how to fix that. My father got to cut off a lot of arms. I want to cut off arms, too. I'll be good at that."

"Better at that than at shooting, I hope. Certainly couldn't be worse."

"What's in that shoulder bag, boy?"

The sound of their voices got louder as they egged each other on.

Rafi glanced quickly from side to side, hoping for an escape. All he could see were empty streets.

He could not outrun men in a truck who had guns.

Then, rising from behind the soldiers, Rafi saw a yellow balloon. Then a green balloon, then a red balloon, then a whole giant bouquet of balloons.

The balloons bobbed in the air with all the gentleness of a camel out for a Saturday stroll.

Rafi stared at them. By the time the Taliban soldiers

saw that they did not have his full attention, the balloon seller was rounding the front of their truck. He stood beside Rafi and put a gentle hand on Rafi's shoulder.

"You found my grandson for me," the man said. "Wonderful."

"This boy belongs to you?"

"He is the son of my son."

"And where is your son?"

"Killed by the murderous soldiers of the previous government. But now you have liberated us. God rest his soul."

"God rest his soul," repeated some of the Talibs in a respectful murmur.

"Is this true, boy?"

"You will have to forgive him," the man said. "He does not talk much. Ever since he saw..." The balloon seller let the sentence trail off.

Whatever the Talibs added to the story in their own minds, it worked.

"I would like to thank you for your kindness to him," said the balloon seller. "Would you accept this small gift from me?" He separated an orange balloon from the others and handed it to the nearest Talib. "Tie it to your truck," he suggested. "It will help you celebrate your victory."

The Talib took the balloon and held the string tight in his hand. He gave his hand a little jerk and seemed to marvel at how the balloon danced in the air. Then he noticed he was being watched and put some gruff in his voice.

"It's almost curfew," the Talib said. "Get off the streets. And tell the boy not to run. People will think he's a thief."

The truck full of Taliban drove off. Rafi watched the orange balloon get smaller as they got farther away.

"Are you a friend of Mrs. Weera?" he asked the balloon seller.

"I do not know a Mrs. Weera," the man said. "Are you lost? You look lost."

Rafi started to cry, then stopped himself and dried his eyes with his sleeve.

"I'm trying to get home, and I don't even know how to leave Kabul."

"You'd better come home with me," the man said. "Spend the night with my family. It's not safe to be out after curfew."

Since he didn't know what else to do, and he was afraid of running into the Taliban again, Rafi went with the balloon seller.

They went down an alley and then down an alley off that alley. It became a dirt path between mud walls. Tattered curtains hung from doorways. Rafi saw a little dirt-covered child who smiled at him as he passed. He heard a rooster and the cooing of pigeons. An open sewer ran in a stream along the mud-packed walk.

The balloon seller stopped in front of a red and blue

striped curtain with more holes than fabric. He reached across the sewer stream and held back the curtain.

"You are welcome," he said to Rafi.

Rafi hopped across the stream, through the doorway and into a small courtyard. The balloon seller followed, gently bringing the balloons through the door with him.

Two small girls and a boy Rafi's age smiled widely at the sight of their father, then eyed Rafi with suspicion. Rafi said hello and told them his name.

He was used to little ones. He knelt down in front of the girls.

"Your grandfather saved me from some bad men," he said. "Is it all right if I come here for a little visit?"

The girls looked at their grandfather, who nodded. They looked back at him. They didn't smile, but Rafi thought they would not mind if he stayed for a bit. He stood up and looked at the boy, and at the worried look on the boy's face.

"I am not in any trouble," Rafi said. "I'm just trying to get home."

"There's not enough..." the boy started to say.

"It will be fine, Farooq," said the balloon seller. "We will make it work. Let's put on the kettle."

He handed the boy the balloons. Rafi watched the boy count them.

"I gave one to the Taliban," the balloon seller said.

The boy looked at Rafi, and from the look on the boy's face, Rafi could tell he thought his grandfather had gotten the bad end of the bargain.

"A life for a balloon, Farooq," said the balloon seller. "We will manage. The sun will rise tomorrow."

Farooq did not argue. He tied the balloons to a metal railing, then led the way into the house.

Their home was one small room. There were thin mats on the floor and walls made out of mud brick. It smelled of damp. There was a sort of small stove at one end that looked like it had been put together from scraps of other things.

My father would know how to build stoves like that, Rafi thought.

Rafi took in the school uniform hanging from a wooden rafter, inside a plastic sheet. He saw the family's few belongings arranged neatly on shelves made from packing crates.

The little girls tore up pieces of paper that looked like they had been scrounged from garbage on the street. Farooq took them, struck a match and blew on the fire softly to keep it going. He added strips off an old biscuit box and then sticks — small at first, then slightly bigger. There was no great pile of firewood here. Not like there had been at Green Valley.

Farooq goes out every day, Rafi somehow knew. *That's one of his jobs, to find things to burn. And when he is out, and his grandfather is out, the little girls are left alone. And if he doesn't find anything to burn, they have no fire.*

And if their grandfather sells no balloons, they

don't eat.

Rafi had never bought a balloon himself, but his father had bought him one the day they went to the Kabul amusement park. Rafi didn't know how much his father had paid. In his mind, he saw the Afghani notes being handed over and a yellow balloon handed to him in exchange.

Was the cost of one balloon enough to buy bread? Rice? Onions?

When the man gave the balloon to the Taliban to save Rafi, he had been giving away the children's supper.

Rafi's hand went into his shoulder bag to bring out the packets of nuts and dried fruit, but he stopped. If he gave them food, he would make them feel like they were not good hosts. It would be an insult.

Farooq got the fire to catch the sticks. The water in the pot started to steam. He poured it into a teapot.

The family owned three cups. Rafi, as the guest, was given his own cup to drink from. The two girls shared one, and Farooq shared with his grandfather.

The tea was weak, but hot and good. There were pieces of stale nan. Rafi ate one, but passed on a second, claiming to be full.

After supper, the little room quickly grew dark. They had no electric light, and not enough trash to keep the fire burning. There were no books, no computers, no television, no garden to sit in, no playground to play in.

There was just sitting. In the dark.

Rafi racked his brain for something to say.

He knew lots of stories from books. Would they like to hear one? He could tell them about the movies he'd seen or sing them one of Aunt Maryam's songs, or tell them about how it was possible to cover whole blocks in New York City by jumping from roof to roof.

Surely at least one of those things would be amusing to this family, and he could repay them for their kindness.

But just as he opened his mouth to speak, Farooq spoke.

He began to recite from the Holy Qur'an, verse after verse.

He went on and on in a quiet, melodic voice. Rafi's jaw dropped.

Farooq had memorized so much!

When Farooq stopped, one of the little girls recited a much shorter passage, followed by another short passage from her sister. Then the grandfather picked up the recitation for a few passages and passed it back to Farooq. Farooq recited more, then taught a new verse to his sisters.

Rafi was not pressured to recite. He was able to just sit and listen to the words that had brought comfort and strength to millions of people over the centuries. The sacred words danced around him and made him know he was a part of something great and wondrous.

He slept next to Farooq in the musty room, under

a quilt that smelled of smoke. He was awakened by coughing in the early hours of the morning.

He lay awake, waiting for the cougher to settle and for all to get quiet again.

He slipped out from under the quilt, put his grandfather's shoulder bag across his back, and lifted his shoes from the entranceway.

The lavatory was a shed in a corner of the yard. Feeling around the walls in the dark, Rafi found a nail protruding from the rough wood of the doorframe.

He reached under his shirt and took off one of his aunt's gold chains, a treasure that came from the music she made and that the balloon seller's family could turn into food, fuel and things that would make their lives easier.

He hung the chain on the nail.

Then he took out a pen and the old copy of *To Kill a Mockingbird*. Gently, quietly, he tore out the front page, the one with more space than words.

On it, he wrote, *Thank you*.

He impaled the note on the nail. Then he silently left the yard.

He hoped he had done the right thing. Sometimes it was hard to know.

23

Parvana lifted her burqa and welcomed the cool night air on her face.

She was no longer alone in the little thicket. A family of seven was camped out nearby.

"Would you be all right if we stayed over here?" the man had asked her respectfully, when they arrived just before sunset.

Parvana pointed out the Taliban flag, visible behind what used to be her gate.

"Right under their noses, eh?" the man said. "Might be the safest place in the whole country. Would you mind if we stayed? Just until we can make other arrangements."

Parvana nodded and gestured that they were welcome, but she did not speak. She could always talk later. For now she wanted to listen and watch and wait. It was actually better for her that the new family was there. It would be easier for her to disappear in a group.

She was seated with her back against the largest of the trees. Its branches hung down to meet the younger trees growing up and the high weeds among the saplings. Tucked under her burqa was a bag with snacks, water, a notebook and pen, and a cell phone. Shauzia would call in the morning to let her know how far the group had gotten.

And Rafi—maybe Rafi would find a way to call her and let her know where he was.

Every hour or so, Parvana stood up and moved around just enough to keep her blood flowing and her legs from cramping. The burqa gave her privacy when she had to relieve herself in the tall weeds, twenty paces or so from her watching place.

The family near her were not used to living rough. They couldn't figure out how to hang a blanket for shelter. They could not get comfortable on the ground. They exchanged harsh words about whether it had been necessary to leave when they had. Maybe they could have been comfortable for one more week! Two more weeks! How long could they be expected to live like beggars in the dirt?

Parvana actually smiled when she heard that.

People get used to comfort, she thought. *It's better to be used to discomfort.*

Comfort was unusual for Parvana. She'd had comfort in Green Valley and a few other places over the years, but it never felt real or solid. Always, it felt like a holiday that would end and would leave her sitting in the shadows and watching out for enemies.

She had fed her family when she was a girl and the Taliban had said, "No girls on the street!" She had defied them and her family had lived. She had been in a cell on an American military base and had kept her tongue and her sanity under what some would call torture but what others would simply call life under occupation.

She had been through things.

So, she could sit in the dirt for a few days and wait for her son.

And if Rafi did not show up?

There would have to be a limit to her waiting. She could not spend the rest of her life sitting under a tree like a burqa-clad Buddha.

She flipped the burqa back down to cover her face.

She hadn't reached her waiting limit yet.

24

Damsa was sleeping on a mattress so soft, and under a blanket so thick and cozy, she was like a caterpillar in a cocoon.

And then she woke up. Still in Afghanistan.

Her face was wet from drizzle that was still falling. A sharp rock pressed into the small of her back. Larmina's elbow poked into her cheek. On the other side of her, Hadiah's foot was plopped on her calf.

Damsa felt like she had been asleep for only five minutes. She'd had a long night of trying—and failing—to get comfortable.

Tired though she was, Damsa knew that sleep had left her for good. She couldn't lie there one second longer. She had to find some stretching room.

The Green Valley group was so tightly packed together that waking up one person would have meant waking up all of them. Then all the others would wake up. The noise and the chores would start, and Damsa really needed some time to herself.

Slowly, silently, she wriggled away from the sleeping group on the ground and rose to her feet. As she did, she could see the carpet of people covering the whole clearing. Smoke rose from smoldering cook fires. The dampness in the air made her even more thirsty.

When they had arrived late yesterday, Damsa had been too busy to notice much beyond what was needed to get the immediate chores done, like unpacking blankets and finding out where to go to the bathroom. She'd gone with Hadiah to look for water, but all they found was a stagnant pond, too dangerous to drink from.

"You'll get sick," Hadiah warned a family who drank straight from the pond, cupping the greenish water with their hands.

"We get sick from drinking or we die from thirst," said the woman.

"At least boil it first."

"You want us to boil it? Give us a pot and some firewood or go away."

They went away.

The only water they could use was the water they carried with them. They had to be careful because they didn't know how long it would have to last. Everyone had to drink. Only the baby got washed, if a quick scrubbing with a damp cloth could be called a wash.

Damsa carefully picked her way through the tiny campsites families had set up. Some families had staked out their territory, placing stones in a circle around their space or stacking tree branches around it to make a nest. Damsa wasn't able to walk in a straight line.

Minutes in, she started to worry that she wouldn't be able to find her way back to the others.

She turned around and scanned the field until she saw her group. They were between a pink flowered blanket hanging from a tree branch and a cardboard hut with an orange tarp for a roof.

"Pink blanket, orange roof," Damsa mumbled, hoping she wouldn't forget. She carried on, tiptoeing around sleeping people and their carefully stacked belongings.

She went out to the weeds far from people and went to the bathroom. That done, she climbed a small hill and looked down at the camp below. She ran her hands through her cropped hair, trying to rub out some of the dust and pebbles her head had rolled around in all night.

Her brain was foggy with unslept sleep. A headache thumped behind her eyes. She wanted a hot shower. She wanted soft-boiled eggs and fresh, warm nan dripping with honey.

There was enough light in the sky now that she could see how big this camp was. It stretched all along the open valley and into a thick stand of trees. Damsa wondered if there was a river running through those trees, a place where they could all get clean and refill their water bottles.

She pulled herself up onto a large boulder and sat. It was almost peaceful there. She was far enough away to be beyond the stench and the worst of the noise of crying babies and the camp waking up, but close enough to watch life unfold like a pageant before her.

She saw people bending low, greeting the day with prayers. She watched a row of small children trying to squirm away from a determined mother with a facecloth. She saw a tall man stoop over as he walked beside a toddler who clutched at his fingertips. She watched old women fan small fires to life with pieces of cardboard, and children playing kickball with a rock.

She heard babies crying, people coughing, the bang of pots being found among the baggage, and saw precious water poured from bottles to make tea.

What will all these people eat? Damsa wondered.

Some, like the Green Valley folks, would have food with them, whatever they had been able to scrounge. But that food wouldn't last forever.

Damsa's mouth felt like it was full of old socks, but they had toothpaste and toothbrushes with them. Already she had mastered the art of brushing her teeth with a pinch of paste and a smidgen of water, but what would they do when the toothpaste ran out?

Would she ever be clean again? Would she ever sleep on a mattress and have enough food and be able to plan for her future without feeling like a dreaming fool?

"You're on my rock."

Damsa was startled.

A woman with a flipped-back burqa showing her wrinkled face and missing teeth glared at Damsa.

"That's my rock. I always sit there in the mornings. Ask anyone. It's mine."

"There are other rocks," said Damsa.

"Go find yourself one, then. This one's mine. Has been for months. Everybody knows it."

"Months?" Damsa asked "You've been here for months?"

"And this is my rock. So get off it."

Damsa climbed down off the boulder.

"How long are you going to stay here?" she asked the woman.

"You want this rock, you'll have to wait until I die. Now go away. I want some privacy."

Damsa left the woman on her rock. As she walked away, she heard the woman still saying, "Everyone knows this rock is mine. Always has been. Everyone knows it."

Damsa felt herself start to tremble as she headed back into the camp. She could feel it in her legs, her arms, her hands and her heart.

"Pink blanket, orange roof. Pink blanket, orange roof," she chanted as she walked.

She made it back to the Green Valley group. Her legs buckled under her and she collapsed to the ground. Old Mrs. Musharef took one look at her, then handed her the baby.

While the rest of the group did chores around her, Damsa held baby Lara until the waves of panic rolled away.

25

Blocks from the balloon seller's house, Rafi wanted to turn around.

Why hadn't he stayed with that family? Maybe they could have introduced him to other balloon sellers, and maybe one of them could have helped him get home.

But he had left, and he doubted he could find his way back to that same alley with that same doorway. There was nothing to do but keep going forward.

He hoped he was going forward. He still didn't know if he was leaving the city or going deeper into the heart of it. Green Valley was to the south and to the west of Kabul. Getting home shouldn't be this hard. But Kabul was a big city, and Rafi felt like a very small boy. The streets were all strange to him.

Rafi kept walking because he didn't know what else to do. He turned down yet another street full of closed-up shops. The street looked familiar. Was it because he had walked along it before, or because all city streets with closed shops looked the same?

He sat on the curb with his feet in the street and his back against a lamp post. He was tired and hungry and scared.

He couldn't keep wandering like this forever. Something had to be different today. He needed to think.

Once he started thinking, the tears started to fall. The horrible scene at the airport kept flashing in his mind—the stench of the sewer water that he could still smell on himself, the noise of the explosion, the search for bodies.

Finding his father.

He sobbed openly now, crying in gulps as he tried to breathe and cry at the same time. All the while, in the back of his mind, he wondered what the point was. He was crying because he was sad, but if no one was there to hear him and tell him it was going to be okay, what was the point of all those tears? Why cry at all? He would be just as sad when he finished crying, and his father would be just as dead.

All the same, point or no point, Rafi cried on, his head in his hands, his face lowered.

Something rattle-zoomed by him in the street.

By the time he raised his head, whatever it was that had zoomed past him was gone.

But then it came back.

A teenaged boy in jeans and a long-sleeved T-shirt rolled by him on a bicycle and circled in for a closer look before giving a sharp whistle through his teeth.

Another kid on a bike joined him, and then three more. They built up speed, jumped up on the curbs and down again. They pedaled circles around Rafi.

Rafi couldn't keep crying when this was going on! He didn't even want to.

He stood up and watched the older boys zip by with control and confidence on two wheels.

One by one, they came to a stop in front of Rafi.

"Why are you crying, kid?" one of the boys asked.

"I'm not crying," Rafi said, and which he could truthfully say at that moment.

"Nah. He's not crying," said another of the boys. "He's got it all together, don't you?"

"Is this where you live, beside this lamppost?"

"No," said Rafi. "I live at Green Valley."

"Never heard of it."

The boy straightened the wheels of his bike.

"If you don't live here, you'd better leave," the boy said. "The Taliban will get you. They come down here all the time looking for looters. You've parked yourself outside a jewelry store!"

Rafi looked at the line of shuttered shops. He was in a gold market.

"What are *you* doing here, then?" Rafi asked them. "Won't the Taliban get you, too?"

"Those old men?"

With that, the bikers took off in a rattle-zoom down the street.

Rafi was alone again.

I need to pay attention, he thought. *No more sitting with my eyes closed.*

That's what would be different today. He would pay better attention to what was around him, and he would be bolder about asking people for help. Kabul was a big city but it wasn't an infinite city. There was a way out of it. He could pay attention to which hills the sun set behind. That, at least, would be west.

He would find a way home today. He would not let any more grown-ups get away with saying they couldn't help him.

"There's nothing like a good strong decision to get your feet moving," Aunt Shauzia loved to say. Rafi's feet took him quickly away from the gold market.

He soon found himself in a wealthy residential area. The streets were clean and there were flower gardens in the center boulevard.

Many of the homes had furniture piled outside their walls. Rafi saw tables, sofas, mattresses and bed frames.

A large man was tossing some of the belongings into the back of a pickup truck. Not all of them. He was sorting through the furniture and household things and taking only what he wanted.

Rafi walked over to him. Here was a man with a truck. If this man couldn't actually take him home, he should at least be able to point Rafi in the right direction.

"What are you staring at?" the man asked him. "I am not stealing, if that's what you are thinking."

The man lifted a chair into his truck.

"All of this stuff is abandoned. Its owners tried to sell it but no one is buying. They all want to leave Afghanistan. They're heading for the border. So if you're one of their spies, spy on someone else. I am not doing anything wrong."

"One of whose spies?" Rafi asked.

"Our new lords and masters. Who, incidentally, are also our old lords and masters. May they be less trouble to a humble businessman like me than the crooks they kicked out." With this last statement, the man raised his arms to heaven.

"I'm not a spy," said Rafi.

"You're not hungry enough yet." The man picked up a small table, examined it and put it in the truck. "When you're hungry enough, you'll sell out your own mother.

"Look at all these things," the man continued, pointing at boxes of dishes and a set of glass tea tables. "People spent their money. They made careful choices. They invited their friends over to their homes so they could say, 'Look at us, how rich we are, how sure of ourselves we are. Our world will never crumble because we have all these things!' And where are they now? Sitting on their suitcases in long lines at the border, waiting to get into a different country where they hope they will have fewer problems. But you know what? Problems always find us."

"You don't like things," Rafi said. "So why are you putting them in your truck?"

"Because I like to eat," said the man. "I know a shop that will sell these for me and give me a cut of the sale price."

"So some people still want these things," said Rafi.

"I hope so," said the man. "Otherwise I've wasted gas money driving here and back to Kala."

Kala. Rafi remembered seeing a sign with that name on it on the drive into Kabul.

"I can help you load the truck," Rafi said. "Take me with you to Kala. I'm trying to get home."

"I don't need help and I'm not a taxi service."

The man got in his truck and drove a short way down the street to the next pile of stuff.

Rafi crossed the street and kept watch, out of the man's line of sight. When he heard the truck door shut again, Rafi ran to the truck and scrambled into the back. He kept his head down as the truck, loaded with other people's abandoned treasures, picked up speed and left the neighborhood.

There were more cars on the road now, and the stop and start of traffic made Rafi's heart stop and start, too.

So what if the driver catches me, he thought. *He's bigger than me but I can outrun him.*

And with every rotation of the truck's tires, Rafi was closer to home.

26

66 Women will not be silent! Women will not be silent!"

"Get out of the way!"

The man driving the furniture truck yelled out his window. The chants did not stop.

"Women will not be silent! Women will not be silent!"

Women were protesting.

In a flash, Rafi was out of the truck and running toward the rally.

He stopped right in the middle of it and grinned.

He had not felt so much at home since he'd left home.

There were maybe fifty women, most with their faces showing. They held placards with slogans like *Women's Rights Are Human Rights* and *We Are Half the World*. They were marching in a circle, slowing down traffic and taking up a lot of space.

Rafi went up to the nearest protestor.

"Are you a Friend of Mrs. Weera?"

The woman shook her head and kept chanting.

He went to the next woman.

"Are you a Friend of Mrs. Weera?"

Another no, and two more after that.

The next woman he asked had long, graying hair pulled off her face and mostly hidden by a bright blue headscarf.

"Are you a Friend of Mrs. Weera?"

The woman stopped chanting and looked down at Rafi.

"Are you?" Rafi asked again. "Are you a Friend of Mrs. Weera?"

He could swear she was about to nod when the area was swamped with pickup trucks and motorbikes, all loaded with Taliban.

"Go back to your homes!" the Taliban yelled.

The women yelled louder. "Respect the rights of women! Respect the rights of women!"

The Taliban men swung at the protestors with whips and clubs. Rafi saw blood on a woman's face. He saw another woman fall to the ground. He ran to help her up, but other protesters got to her first and hurried her away.

Placards dropped to the ground as the women went in many directions, making it difficult for the Taliban to keep track of them.

Rafi was frantic. He could no longer see that older woman in the blue headscarf. He dashed around the intersection, looking all around, until he spotted her.

She was with two younger women, all walking quickly away from the scene. Rafi ran after them. He saw them turn a corner. He got to that corner himself just in time to see them turn another corner.

When he got to where they had turned, there was no one to be seen. Just a cement alley with high walls and closed gates.

Rafi was all done being alone. He desperately needed help and he needed it now.

"Does anybody know Mrs. Weera?" he called out at the top of his voice.

A door opened behind him. He turned around.

The blue-scarf woman from the rally was there.

"How do you know Mrs. Weera?" she asked quietly.

"My mother used to work with her," Rafi told her.

"And what is your mother's name?"

"Parvana."

The woman stepped out into the alley, grabbed Rafi and pulled him into her yard. She closed the alley door and bent down to look at him.

"You're Parvana's son?"

Rafi nodded.

He found himself crushed in a big hug.

"Your mother saved me after I escaped the massacre in Mazar-e-Sharif, many years ago," the woman said when she finally released him. "She was your age then. My name is Homa."

Homa took him into her house.

"This is Parvana's son," she exclaimed to the group of people gathered there. "This is Parvana and Asif's boy!"

In an instant, Rafi was surrounded by people greeting him, embracing him, turning him his way and that and expressing amazement at him showing up at their door. They told him how much they admired his parents. They examined him for Parvana's determined forehead and Asif's kind eyes. They asked him question after excited question about why he was alone and how he had managed to find them.

Rafi was getting dizzy with relief and with all the questions when an arm reached in through the happy group and pulled him out.

It was a boy his age.

"Give him some air," the boy said to the adults, who laughed and agreed and talked about making tea.

The boy led Rafi down the hall.

"Kids know what kids need."

He opened a door. Rafi looked inside. The kid was right. Rafi needed a bathroom.

"Hold on," the boy said. In a flash, he left and returned with a clean, folded shalwar kameez. He handed it to Rafi.

"Take your time," the boy said. "I'll handle the mob." He grinned and left Rafi in peace.

When Rafi rejoined the group, he smelled of flowers instead of sewage.

His soiled shalwar kameez was whisked away to be washed, and Rafi was welcomed to a spot on a toshak. Tea and bread, walnuts and candied almonds were laid before him. He so wanted to eat but felt self-conscious with so many strange grown-ups staring at him.

The boy helped him out again, tearing off a piece of nan and asking if he played football.

"When I can," Rafi said. He ate and drank and they talked about the benefits of various positions on the field, and then Rafi noticed a funny silence among the adults in the room.

The football talk trailed off.

"I talked to your mother," Homa said. "She is all right. She's waiting for you at Green Valley. She wants to talk to you whenever you're ready."

The bread stuck in Rafi's throat. He sipped some tea to help it go down.

"Shall I call her now?" Homa asked. "Do you want to talk to her?"

Rafi nodded.

A phone was brought out. Homa spoke quietly into it. Then she handed it to him.

Rafi vaguely heard the boy talking to the adults to try to distract them from watching him, but mostly he heard his mother's voice, soothing in that special direct way of hers. It reassured him that she had everything under control, and he would be all right.

He couldn't speak his response, only nod.

He handed the phone back to Homa. She listened to Parvana, replied, then ended the call.

"You are to eat as much as you can hold," Homa told Rafi. "Then, when you're ready, we will get you back to your mother."

"I'm ready now," Rafi said.

"Your mother said you were to eat first. Do you want to disobey Parvana?"

More food was brought out. Everyone gathered around the dining cloth spread on the floor and ate warmed-up leftover chicken and rice along with cucumber salad.

Rafi looked at the protest signs leaning against the door frame. He saw the women's rights and environmental justice posters on the walls, and the stacks of leaflets on a table. He listened to reports of the protest.

Someone said, "Remember that time Mrs. Weera forced that drug lord to open up a community center in the heart of his slum district?"

Someone else said, "Remember that time we helped Parvana get a whole family of girls away from that awful man? He was an awful man, Rafi. He'd beat them with firewood. I wonder if we'll still be able to open that drug treatment facility with the Taliban back in power."

"Rafi," said Homa, "when your mother was a child she decided who she wanted to be and she never wavered from that. She could have left me in that bombed-out building where she found me. I had no burqa, it was after curfew and Kabul was crawling with Taliban. She could have turned away from me but she didn't. I don't think she's ever turned away from anyone in her whole life."

"We try to be like her," added a man.

Rafi listened to them talk, and he ate until he could eat no more.

"You're full?" Homa asked. "Now we can get you back to your mother."

Rafi stayed where he was while the adults cleaned up the sitting room and packed up food for him to take. The boy moved closer to him and sat.

"My name's Laith," he said. "I lost my father, too. Three years ago. We don't know who killed him—the government or the Taliban or someone else. It's awful. But it gets easier. Some days."

A motor revved outside.

"What's that?" Rafi asked, startled.

"Your ride," Laith said with a grin.

They got to their feet. Homa bustled around him.

"Now, here is food that should be eaten no later than tomorrow. This other package is food that will keep a few days longer. Here are several bottles of water and here are a few water-purification tablets. And here is your shalwar kameez, still damp from washing but it won't take long to dry in the sun once you get back to your mother. No, no, you can keep the one you've got on. Laith has others."

They went out into the yard.

"This is Yousef," Homa said. "He's the father of one of our members. He'll take you home."

Yousef, a tall, older man in traditional dress and a long beard, put his hand on his heart and bowed his head slightly in greeting. Then he stepped to one side to reveal his vehicle.

He was taking Rafi home on a motorcycle.

Rafi grinned so widely he thought his face would break.

Just wait until his mother saw him ride up on that!

27

Damsa guided one adult, two teenagers, ten children (they'd picked up four abandoned young brothers along the way) and one baby up the broken staircase of the broken school.

Old Mrs. Musharef had begged off, even though she insisted her ankle was fine. She'd twisted it along the road nearly a week ago, necessitating this rest stop.

"At my age, I've got no business climbing stairs I don't need to climb," she said.

Damsa was pretty sure Old Mrs. Musharef needed a break from all of them more than she needed a break from the stairs.

"Be careful of this sharp bit," Damsa warned everyone.

A piece of broken rebar stuck out of a chunk of concrete like a chocolate curl out of an ice-cream cone she'd once had. Everyone gave it a wide berth. When one of the smaller children reached out to touch it, Hadiah pulled the little arm away.

They all made it to the landing. Damsa, holding the baby, led them up the rest of the stairs. Any moment now, they'd be able to see what she came up here every evening to see.

And then they saw it.

A collective "Ahhhhh" sounded out.

Big chunks of the walls of the top floor of the school had been blown out by a bomb years ago. One open wall framed a view of the mountains to the west, with the sky beginning to tinge red with the coming sunset.

Everyone was on the top floor now. Shauzia used her policewoman voice.

"Get into your squads."

The children loved this game. They formed three lines of three in front of Shauzia, with Hadiah at her side as her deputy. The squads were a mixture of boys and girls.

"Report on the environment," Shauzia ordered.

"A hole in the floor to the right," said a boy.

"Another hole in the floor to the left," reported one of the girls.

"I see broken glass over there," pointed the youngest of the boys, who didn't know his left and his right yet.

"Big holes in the walls," said one of his brothers, "and no railings."

"Are we looking for trouble?" Shauzia asked.

"No, Sheriff Shauzia," they replied.

"Are we going to take care of everyone in our squad?"

"Yes, Sheriff Shauzia!"

"Off you go, then," Shauzia said. "Have fun. And try not to make too much noise. People here have had a long day and could use a quiet evening."

Damsa had to smile. It was never quiet in the school.

The bottom two floors were chock-full of families. Some, like the Green Valley group, were in their own rooms. Damsa thought their tiny space might have once been the principal's office. It had a broken clock on one wall along with a picture of Mecca and a map of the world. The map was very old. It still had the USSR on it.

Other families shared larger classrooms, stringing up blankets on ropes to provide a bit of privacy.

So far, one of the classrooms remained empty, a place for people to pray and children to play. Every other inch of the school was used as a home for someone.

Except for the top floor.

With so many holes in the floor and walls open to the sky, broken glass and twisted, rusty rebar, it was too dangerous for playing and way too dangerous for sleeping—someone might fall through a hole as they stumbled around in the darkness. Instead, it was a semi-quiet haven for those brave enough to climb the broken stairs.

Damsa had been coming up here every evening after chores to watch the sunset and claim some time for herself. If any of the others had wanted to join her, they had kept that to themselves and let her have her time.

They would all be leaving in the morning. Damsa really wanted to share this view with everyone on their last night in the school.

Deputy Hadiah kept an eye on the squads as they quietly, carefully explored the big empty space.

It must have been an indoor playground and assembly room at one time. There were classrooms along one wall, but the rest of the space was open. Hopscotch games were painted on the floor. Giant ducks and bunnies and quotations from the Qur'an about the pursuit of knowledge were painted on the walls. Minnie Mouse was there, too, but only half of her. The other half had been blown away.

Damsa's group had the whole floor almost to themselves that evening. A small group of women sat in one corner. Damsa heard enough of what they were saying to guess that they were teaching each other to read.

A man was alone in another corner, drawing on the floor with pieces of charcoal.

"I'll bet this was a good school," said Larmina. She sat with Shauzia and Zahra on a big chunk of concrete close enough to the open wall to be a window seat but not so close to be dangerous for them to sit on. "I'll bet the teachers were friendly and the kids were happy and their parents were proud of what they learned."

"Is that where we're going?" Zahra asked, pointing at the mountains, now a glowing, fiery red from the setting sun.

"It is," said Shauzia.

"How will we get there?"

"We'll get there," replied Shauzia, calm and sure.

"What about Parvana?" asked Zahra. "How will she find us?"

"She'll find us," said Shauzia, without a note of doubt in her voice.

They stopped talking then and just watched as the earth spun and made the sun seem to sink lower in the sky. It followed a path where it went down between two mountains, lighting up the whole ridge and creating an arc of brilliant color that bounced off a long, thin spatter of clouds above.

The mountains seemed close, but Damsa knew they were still many days of difficult travel away.

She took a step closer to the open wall and looked down.

Just below, the market was packing up for the night.

Stretched out along the old playground, people with something to sell displayed their things on blankets and old newspapers. Most sold household things, fancy clothes and family treasures they thought they couldn't do without when they left their homes but provided little use on their current journey. Few of the travelers had money to spare for the watches, tea sets, lapis rings or silk shalwar kameez, but the market gave everyone something to do and a place to gather and gossip.

Those who had a bit of money trekked the three miles into the village and bought bread, nuts and dried fruit and then resold them at the school for slightly higher prices.

"Enough to make a profit," the bread seller told Damsa earlier that morning when she'd bought bread from him for the group, "but not so much that people will think we are being greedy and taking advantage of them."

"Very wise," Damsa replied. "Who needs more enemies these days?"

"Exactly," said the bread seller, and he handed over the nan.

As the sun dipped lower, Damsa thought of all the things she could do now that she had never even thought of doing in her old life. She could have a good sleep on hard ground. She could keep young children safe in traffic. She could walk and walk and still have energy at the end of the day to set up camp.

The younger ones completed their explorations of the room and gathered around the open wall to watch the sunset. Damsa saw the orange light shine on their faces. The children all looked magnificent.

She remembered the vision she once had of herself, in a bright shiny laboratory, wearing a spotless white coat. She might still be able to get that. Who knew what would happen in the future?

"I beg your pardon," said a voice behind them.

They turned to see the man who had been drawing. He was standing a few paces back. He gave them a gentle bow.

"Before the light disappears, I would like to invite you all to see what I have been drawing," he said.

The women from the reading group were already over there, standing in a semicircle and looking at the floor, pointing down and talking quietly.

Damsa and her group joined them.

"I am calling it *The Garden of Afghanistan*," the artist said.

It was a garden that he had drawn. On rough cement with only charcoal, he had created a vision of their country as they all knew it could be, even though many of them were not yet old enough to know that they knew.

There were orchards and snow leopards, playgrounds and schools, women and men and children learning and building together.

"I'd like to live there," said Noosala.

"We will," said Shauzia, as strong and sure and steady as the mountains.

28

Parvana sat on the ledge outside the cave under a cloudy sky.

Below her was the village with its mud homes, scattered shops and small graveyard. It was surrounded by the brown-yellow earth of early winter. A small flock of fat-tailed sheep grazed on tufts of greenery. They were watched over by a young shepherd.

It was late in the afternoon. Parvana hoped he had supper waiting for him.

Hunger was a real problem in this Afghanistan. She and Rafi had seen many children on the brink of starvation. They'd given what they could to the families, but Parvana knew it wasn't enough, and that many would die over the winter.

Of course it bothered her. She hated her limitations. For every girl she saved, there were hundreds more forced into marriages they didn't want. For every child Parvana taught to read, there were a thousand who would never hold a book. For every person she fed, there were so many others who would die empty in the cold and the dark.

That was life these days in Afghanistan. That was life in many countries, even in this modern world that had glorious technology, unlimited access to knowledge and many kind people who wanted to do good. Some people were still considered expendable. That's the way it was. That's just what she had to fight against.

There was a small break in the clouds. A stream of bright sunlight hit the graveyard. Parvana looked at the gravestones gleaming white in the sudden sunshine.

It reminded her of a similar sunbeam shining on a similar graveyard back when she and Shauzia were children, digging up human bones to sell to a bone broker. Their families ate that night, but the images of the skulls they unearthed would sometimes come to her in her dreams, to stare at her and remind her that she had disturbed their rest.

"Fat chance of finding rest in Afghanistan," Parvana whispered to them now. "Why should you get to be at peace? No one else is."

Then she laughed at herself for such a bitter statement. She was not a bitter woman! In fact, at this moment, she was feeling pretty good.

After a week of hard travel, aided by the Friends of Mrs. Weera, she and Rafi were finally here with the others from Green Valley and a few more besides. Rafi was delighted to have four new brothers, especially since he was older and they looked up to him.

Two more girls had joined them, too—runaways Hadiah's age. She and Rafi had met them along the way. That made twenty in their little cave complex. They still had room for a few more. Shauzia was in touch with some female journalists who were being targeted by the Taliban. They needed a safe place to stay and would arrive in a few days.

Their new cave home had been found for them by one of Shauzia's policewoman friends. The caves had been used by the Soviet army decades ago. They still held a dozen metal cots, empty vodka bottles and a metal footlocker with mess kits, copies of *Pravda* and a collection of hand-carved birds. At the bottom of the box were three sets of woodcarving tools the children could learn to use.

They had also found a bundle of letters with Soviet stamps on the envelopes. Hadiah took possession of them, vowing to learn Russian so she could find out what they said.

Most thought they were love letters. Some thought they might be letters from the soldiers' parents. Rafi suggested that one letter might be an invitation to one of the soldiers to join the Bolshoi Ballet.

Parvana's heart broke when she heard him say that. Asif would have built their son a ballet barre already. She would have to find a way to do that.

Thoughts of Asif filled her with pain. There was nothing to do but live with it. That's what loss did. It hurt. Parvana had lost homes, family and love, but at least she had once had those things. She still had more than most. She appreciated it all every day, knowing that at any moment, it could be snatched from her. They were all, always, seconds away from a bomb, from prison, from death.

Parvana heard laughter coming from inside the cave.

Shauzia joined her on the ledge and handed her a cup of tea.

"Your son is dancing the Dance of the Taliban in the Teacups," Shauzia said.

"He's supposed to be doing fractions."

"There's time for both. He and Larmina are writing a Broadway play. Did he tell you? It's called *The Almond Sheller*, for Maryam to star in, now that she's in New York."

"That will keep her out of trouble," said Parvana.

These young lives she was caring for were such brave, strong souls! Larmina was a mix of poet and psychologist. Hadiah was a scholar without a school, but she would find a way to let her mind soar. The three sisters were loyal and brave. The youngest two girls were soaking up love like flowers soak up sunshine. Zahra and baby Lara would grow strong and know that they had the right to choose what they did with their lives. The four brothers, whose backs bore the scars of a lifetime of beatings, were already showing signs they would grow to be the best of Afghan men — kind, considerate and carrying the pride of the generations of the strong, good men who came before them.

And Damsa — what a surprise that girl had turned out to be! Starting out in a life where everything was given to her, now living rough in a cave, teaching the younger ones, working hard and, by all appearances, having the time of her life.

That's what freedom does for us, Parvana thought.

And her Rafi, full of the goodness of his father and her own stubbornness. Would he ever get to be the dancer he once dreamed of being, or would he have another dream?

I'm only thirty-two, Parvana thought. *Maybe there's still time for me to dream, too.*

"Are you going to build me another Eiffel Tower?" Shauzia asked, interrupting Parvana's thoughts. "Plant me another lavender field?"

"You mean Russian sage?"

"Some call it Afghan lavender."

Parvana drank tea with her old friend and listened to the laughter behind them.

"This is paradise," Parvana said.

"Another Green Valley," said Shauzia.

They were ready for the future, ready for the fight, ready for the pain, and ready for death.

Ready for joy.

"We're alive," said Parvana.

"We're alive," said Shauzia. She took hold of Parvana's hand.

"So let's keep living."

AUTHOR'S NOTE

In August of 2021, the Taliban retook power in Kabul and in the whole of Afghanistan.

Although they were kicked out of power in late 2001, the Taliban never went away. For decades they battled troops from around the world who went to Afghanistan to support the democratically elected government. As these troops went home, and the corruption of some government officials continued, the power of the Taliban grew. This led to the terrible events of August and September, with people crowding the airport and even climbing on the wings of airplanes, desperate to escape.

Understanding Afghanistan's present means knowing its history. In late 1979 the Soviet Union invaded the country, but even after they were defeated in 1989, the fighting continued, as various groups fought for control of the country. The Taliban militia, one of the groups that the United States and Pakistan funded, trained and armed to fight the Soviets, took control of the capital city of Kabul in 1996. They imposed brutal and restrictive laws on girls and women. Schools for girls were closed, women were no longer allowed to hold jobs, and strict dress codes were enforced.

The Taliban also harbored al-Qaeda, the terrorists who were responsible for the September 11th attacks on the United States in 2001. In response, the US led a coalition of nations into a war in Afghanistan.

To speak of Afghanistan means to speak of war, of bombs dropped on villages by drones, of tanks in the streets, of civilians killed and of soldiers lost in battle. Many soldiers back in their home countries around the world carry the trauma of their time in Afghanistan.

To speak of Afghanistan is to speak of refugees. People have fled the decades of violence and oppression, hoping for a chance at a life somewhere kinder. Many are stuck in camps. Many are contributing their talents to their new home countries, even as their hearts ache for their homeland. Many have drowned in the Mediterranean Sea when their overcrowded boats flipped over in the waves.

To speak of Afghanistan is also to speak of the drive of the people there to create a country where beauty and culture and justice flourish.

Several years ago I was privileged to spend some time in Afghanistan interviewing children for a book called *Kids of Kabul*. I met people who took hold of the smallest opportunity for growth and stretched it to create similar opportunities for others. Children who had missed out on school studied hard because no one was sure that the chance for an education would not be taken from them again. Adults who had never gone to school flooded into literacy classes and assisted with bringing the first libraries into their communities. Artists, journalists, athletes, scientists, women-owned small businesses—all sorts of enterprises flourished, even while the country remained at war.

The current Taliban regime has promised to allow girls to go to school and has sworn off the more barbaric punishments they practiced back in the late 1990s. We shall see. So far, their human rights record is not good. As of this writing, the Afghan economy is in freefall, and millions are facing starvation because they cannot afford to buy food. Aid is trickling in, but there is nervousness about whether it will get to the people who need it, and not be used to prop up the Taliban regime.

This is the seventh book I have written about Afghanistan, and the fifth about Parvana. We have seen Parvana grow from a child trying to feed her family into a woman made of iron, like so many Afghan women, fierce in their determination to protect, to build and to create. I love Parvana, Shauzia, Mrs. Weera and Asif. They have been with me for two decades, inspiring me toward the greatness that they carry with them.

No person should be discounted. No one should be underfed. No one should drink poisoned water. No one should be bombed. We have real problems in the world, and we need everyone's brain to solve them—everyone's fed, educated and untraumatized brain.

The retaking of Afghanistan by the Taliban has reminded us that progress does not always move in a straight line. It would be lovely if humanity only got wiser as it got older, but it doesn't always work that way, just as we individuals don't always get wiser with age. Too often we fall back on old patterns, old fears, because they are easier than being brave and reaching out to something new.

Thank you for staying with Parvana all these years. We can honor her by dedicating ourselves to what she wants—a kind world where everyone can become what they are meant to become, without war or prison bars or hunger getting in their way.

Let us be fierce like Parvana and accept nothing less than making the Earth a garden again—beautiful and welcoming to all.

Deborah Ellis
June, 2022

GLOSSARY

al-Qaeda – A network of terrorists who believe in a
  radical, and un-Islamic, version of Islam.
ashak – Afghan dumplings.
burqa – A long tent-like garment worn by women.
  It covers the entire body and has a narrow mesh
  screen over the eyes.
chador – A piece of cloth worn by women and girls
  to cover their hair and shoulders.
Dari – One of the two main languages in
  Afghanistan.
Kabuli rice – An Afghan rice dish.
Logar Province – A province located in eastern
  Afghanistan.
Mecca – A city in Saudi Arabia with deep religious
  significance for Muslims.
nan – Afghan bread, which can be flat, long or
  round.
Pashtu – One of the two main languages in
  Afghanistan.
pattu – A gray or brown woolen blanket shawl
  worn by Afghan men and boys.

Qur'an – Islamic religious text.

Red Crescent – The Muslim equivalent of the Red Cross, an international organization that provides aid to the sick and wounded in times of disaster and war.

refugee – A person who leaves their home due to war, persecution or other danger.

rubab – A lute-like musical instrument.

salaam alaikum – A greeting that means "Peace be unto you" in Arabic. The standard response is walaikum asalaam.

shalwar kameez – Long, loose shirt and trousers, worn by both men and women. A man's shalwar kameez is one color, with pockets in the side and on the chest. A woman's shalwar kameez has different colors and patterns and is sometimes elaborately embroidered or beaded.

Soviets – The people of the Soviet Union before its break-up, including Russia and other Communist countries.

Taliban – A militant group that first took control of Afghanistan in 1996. It was forced from power in 2001 but retook power in 2021.

toshak – A narrow mattress used in many Afghan homes instead of chairs or beds.

USSR – The Union of Soviet Socialist Republics, or the Soviet Union.

The Breadwinner
Deborah Ellis

Eleven-year-old Parvana lives in Kabul, Afghanistan's capital city. Her father works from a blanket on the ground in the marketplace, reading letters for people who cannot read or write. One day he is arrested and the family is left without someone who can earn money or even shop for food.

As conditions for the family grow desperate, only one solution emerges. Forbidden to earn money as a girl, Parvana must disguise herself as a boy, and become the breadwinner.

Recommended by Nobel Peace Prize Winner Malala Yousafzai

"A great kids' book...a graphic geopolitical brief that's also a girl-power parable." —*Newsweek*

"...a book...about the hard times—and the courage—of Afghan children." —*Washington Post*

Baia delle Favole Literary Award • Hackmatack Award • Middle East Book Award • Rebecca Caudill Young Readers' Book Award • Sweden's Peter Pan Prize • YALSA PPYA

Paperback • 978-1-55498-765-8 • $10.99
epub • 978-1-55498-007-9 • $9.95
mobi • 978-1-55498-581-4 • $9.95

Parvana's Journey
Deborah Ellis

A war is raging in Afghanistan as a coalition of Western forces tries to oust the Taliban by bombing the country. Parvana's father has died, and her mother, sister and brother have gone to a faraway wedding. Parvana doesn't know where they are. She just knows she has to find them.

And so, masquerading as a boy, she sets out across the desolate countryside through the war zone that Afghanistan has become.

"Through spare, affecting prose, Ellis ... makes the children's journey both arduous and believable." — *Booklist*

★ "This sequel to *The Breadwinner* easily stands alone... An unforgettable read." — *School Library Journal*, starred review

Jane Addams Children's Book Award • Canadian Library Association Book of the Year for Children Award Honour Book • Governor General's Literary Award Finalist • Manitoba Young Readers' Choice Award • Ontario Library Association Golden Oak Award • Red Cedar Book Award • Ruth Schwartz Award • Amazon.ca Top Ten • YALSA BBYA

Paperback • 978-1-55498-770-2 • $10.99
epub • 978-1-55498-030-7 • $9.95
mobi • 978-1-55498-642-2 • $9.95

Mud City

Deborah Ellis

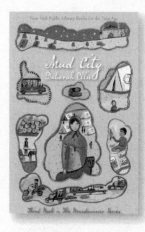

Parvana's best friend, Shauzia, has fled Afghanistan and now has to survive on her own on the streets of Peshawar, Pakistan. With her dog as her only friend, she must scrounge for food, beg for money and look for a safe place to sleep every night.

But could it be worse than a lifetime spent in a refugee camp?

This is a powerful and very human story of a feisty, driven girl who tries to take control of her own life.

★ "A stunning portrait ..." — *Quill & Quire*, starred review

"... a fine, strong addition to Ellis' growing list of novels. Highly recommended." — *Toronto Star*

Hackmatack Award • Lamplighter Award • Cooperative Children's Book Center Choices • New York Public Library Books for the Teen Age

Paperback • 978-1-55498-773-3 • $10.99
epub • 978-1-55498-027-7 • $9.95
mobi • 978-1-55498-690-3 • $9.95

My Name Is Parvana

Deborah Ellis

On a military base in Afghanistan, after the fall of the Taliban in 2001, American authorities have just imprisoned a teenaged girl found in a bombed-out school. The army major thinks the prisoner may be a terrorist. She remains silent even under threats and mistreatment. The only clue to her identity is a tattered bag containing papers that refer to people named Shauzia, Nooria, Leila, Asif, Hassan—and Parvana.

★ "Readers will learn much about the war in Afghanistan even as they cheer on this feisty protagonist."—*Kirkus*, starred review

★ "This sequel to the series is not merely an important book about the difficulty of girls' lives in war-torn, U.S.-occupied Afghanistan. It is also an example of vivid storytelling with a visceral sense of place, loss, distrust, and hope."—*School Library Journal*, starred review

Bank Street College of Education's Best Books of the Year • Cooperative Children's Book Center Choices • Short-listed for the IODE Violet Downey Book Award • Short-listed for the Manitoba Young Readers' Choice Award • USBBY Outstanding International Books

Paperback • 978-1-55498-298-1 • $10.99
epub • 978-1-55498-299-8 • $10.99
mobi • 978-1-55498-628-6 • $10.99

Kids of Kabul:
Living Bravely Through a Never-ending War

Deborah Ellis

What has happened to Afghanistan's children since the fall of the Taliban in 2001? In 2011, Deborah Ellis went to Kabul to find out. The two dozen or so boys and girls featured in this book range in age from ten to seventeen, and they speak candidly about their lives now. They are still living in a country at war. Yet these kids are weathering their lives with remarkable courage and hope, getting as much education and life experience and fun as they can.

"This nuanced portrayal of adolescence in a struggling nation refrains, refreshingly, from wallowing in tragedy tourism and overwrought handwringing. Necessary." — *Kirkus*

★ "... compelling and motivating.... A valuable, informative resource." — *School Library Journal*, starred review

Norma Fleck Award for Canadian Children's Non-Fiction • Joint winner of the South Asia Book Award • Short-listed for the TD Canadian Children's Literature Award • Short-listed for the North Carolina Young Adult Book Award • Bank Street College of Education's Best Books of the Year • IRA Notable Books for a Global Society • USBBY Outstanding International Books

Paperback • 978-1-55498-182-3 • $12.95 CDN / $9.95 US
epub • 978-1-55498-203-5 • $9.95
mobi • 978-1-55498-613-2 • $9.95

DEBORAH ELLIS is the author of almost thirty books for young people. She is best known for her Breadwinner series, which has been published in twenty-five languages. She has won the Governor General's Award, the Middle East Book Award, the Peter Pan Prize, the Jane Addams Children's Book Award and the Vicky Metcalf Award. A recipient of the Order of Canada, Deborah has donated more than $2 million in royalties to organizations such as Canadian Women for Women in Afghanistan, Mental Health Without Borders, the First Nations Child and Family Caring Society of Canada, the Leprosy Mission, Children in Crisis fund of IBBY and the UNHCR. She lives in Simcoe, Ontario.